Rosemary Harris is a Londoner, but spent her early years moving from place to place, 'being slightly educated by different schools. My first stories were dictated when I was about four or five – the central figure was a greyhound, called, oddly enough, Greyhound. He had endless adventures underground by the light of one naked light bulb suspended from a tunnel roof.'

Her first books were for adults and included two thrillers; then in 1968 she published her first children's book – *The Moon in the Cloud* – which was awarded the Library Association's Carnegie Medal. Since then she has written adult thrillers and picture book stories, but she is perhaps best known for her children's novels. These include the two sequels to *The Moon in the Cloud*, *The Shadow on the Sun*, and *The Bright and Morning Star*; the fascinating science fiction sequence *A Quest for Orion* and *Tower of the Stars*; and *Zed*, a powerful story of hostage-taking told from the point of view of the child who is caught up in the drama.

ff

THE SHADOW
ON THE SUN

Rosemary Harris

faber and faber

LONDON · BOSTON

First published in 1970
by Faber and Faber Limited
3 Queen Square London WC1N 3AU
Published by Puffin Books in 1977
This paperback edition first published in 1989
Phototypeset by Input Typesetting Ltd, London

Printed in Great Britain by

All rights reserved

© Rosemary Harris, 1970

A CIP record for this book is available from the British
Library

ISBN 0-571-14185-4

For Ben and Hugh

Contents

Author's Note

The Shadow on the Sun is a sequel to *The Moon in the Cloud*, and tells what happened when Reuben returned to Kemi, the Black Land (Egypt), with his wife Thamar and his animals after the Flood had subsided. Once again the animals never really talk to people – although they naturally speak among themselves – but their language is so well understood by Reuben and Thamar that it's written here as human speech.

The land of Punt was no myth. It truly existed, though no one is quite clear where it was. Some people believe it was the Somaliland coast, others, that it was part of India. Anyway, to the Ancient Egyptians it was a land of strange romance from which all delightful, exotic things came – from dwarfs and incense to ivory and leopard skins. The first records of expeditions there come from the Vth Dynasty – that is, the one before my young (fictional) King Merenkere's.

In placing Punt vaguely somewhere beyond the course of the Blue Nile I have mainly used my imagination, as far as both site and scenery are concerned. Till Reuben and his cat Cefalu cross by the Wadi Hammamat to the Red Sea all is as accurate as possible, but afterwards . . . Well, it's easy to see this is not Lake Tana or Ethiopia, but a land and people which might have equalled some lurid fantasy images in the Ancient Egyptian mind, much as we make our own fantasies in science fiction of life on distant planets.

My people of Punt may not be 'men whose heads do grow beneath their shoulders', but they're equally horrible and unlikely. I plead tolerance for them because of a feeling that the Ancient Egyptians, who, like the White Queen in *Alice* (and ourselves), could gaily believe 'six impossible things before breakfast', might have found them all too credible.

PROLOGUE

Go Down, Reuben . . .

'It's madness!' said Thamar. 'Please, Reuben, forget about it. We could go due south, couldn't we? We could – '

Her husband was absorbed in copying the notes of a bird on his pipe. He trilled excellently and with such grace that the bird's mate came hopping in a gratified way to discover why a love call so potent should be coming from a piece of hollow reed.

'Reuben!'

He lowered the pipe from his lips, and said patiently: 'When the Flood came, it was you who thought it might be only local – who said we could go down to Kemi afterwards and find out if the King and Tahlevi were still alive. Don't you remember, Thamar?'

'I – I wasn't really serious. I was sure Kemi would be flooded too.' She looked at him sideways. 'I just wanted to make you happier.'

Reuben began to play again. She raised her voice. 'Think of the Vizier's hatred, Reuben! Think of Kenamut and – and the High Priest of Sekhmet! You might fall into their hands again.'

3

'I believe the King would be so glad to see me he would protect me – and you – from them all.'

'We've got to reach him first,' said Thamar drily.

'I don't know that it's much safer staying here,' pointed out Reuben, 'now Noah's cursed me for seeing him drunk in his tent, and naked. Sometimes he squints with anger at me. And Shem and Japheth have taken to calling me Reuben again, instead of Ham; and they talk of their wretched brother in a mournful way, as though they loved him dearly before he died, and – '

'And, in fact, the Flood hasn't done all that good after all. Well, only a man would ever have believed it could.'

'Hush, Thamar!' Reuben was scandalized. 'That's blasphemy.'

'It's common sense. Noah only drank now and then before the Flood, but ever since the Ark reached Ararat he's been celebrating. Do you call that an improvement? And one of the tigers has bitten an elephant, and Anak's vanity has grown so enormous since he was one of only two camels saved that his hump as well as his head has swollen. And the poor Indignant Grunk never got on the Ark after all, so we've lost him for ever. I always wanted to see if you could tame a Grunk, and now it's too late.'

'There may be a whole lot of Grunks left down in Kemi,' said Reuben cunningly. 'That is, if the Flood was only a sort of local trial after all.'

'I don't want to go to Kemi.' Thamar was mutinous. 'If it's still there, you'll be killed. We could go – '

4

They were back where they started. Reuben gazed at her, and thought she had grown pigheaded since they were all cooped up together in the Ark. He said so. They were about to have their first quarrel when a diversion was caused by Cefalu, who came strolling up with his unusually long tail curved proud behind him.

'Well,' he said, in the cat language they both understood perfectly, 'have we decided anything?'

'Yes,' said Thamar.

'No,' said Reuben.

They glared at each other. Then Reuben noticed something which turned his thoughts away from Thamar's obstinacy. 'Cefalu, your tail is pleased with itself.'

'Oh, is it?' said Cefalu carelessly. 'It gets like that sometimes. There's no controlling it.' But he smirked a little behind his whiskers.

'Meluseth!' said Thamar suddenly. 'I know, she's had – '

'Five,' Cefalu spoke hurriedly to Reuben before the news could be spoilt. 'Three he-cats and two shes.'

'Clever Cefalu.' Reuben stroked the thick black fur.

'One does one's best.' Cefalu smirked again.

'And Meluseth has done her best,' said Thamar tartly, female sticking up for female. 'Have they long fur, like her, or – '

'Four long, one short.' Cefalu dropped his arrogant posing and became quite simple and natural. 'Meluseth has done well, hasn't she? Noah's wife has given her a medal made from mandrake root, for being the first animal to start the new life rolling. Three sons and two daughters.' He lay down suddenly, frightened.

'Patriarch,' said Reuben fondly; and added, with a piercing look at Thamar, 'The sooner we get down to Kemi out of this mud-strewn wilderness, which will take a long while to support us all properly, the better.'

'We aren't going to Kemi.' But she spoke with less conviction, as Reuben noted.

He looked about him. There was indeed a lot of mud. When a flood goes down it leaves behind it a desolation and end-of-the-worldness that needs to be seen to be understood. They were sitting on a lower slope of Mount Ararat, and beneath them, as far as the eye could see, were rolling plains of mud. Here and there some scrubby bushes thrust up out of the plains, but looked at closer they were only mud bushes, for the stalks and twigs once covered by living leaves had died, and now held waste material which had drifted against them and stuck there, at the bottom of a relentless if temporary sea.

Yet to the east Noah had already planted out a small vineyard; and after planting had been so gloriously wine-filled that the shabby incident when Reuben saw him in his tent had taken place.

'A journey now will need a lot of planning.' Reuben looked at the scene with an experienced eye. 'Supplies, for instance. I suppose the well water will be fresh. Most of the Flood fell from the sky, after all.'

'I wouldn't mind seeing Kemi again, said Cefalu. 'Lovely fresh fish, they had. But Meluseth wishes to present our offspring in the Temple of Ptah, which I do not quite approve. When females are sick they revert to silly ways. She speaks wistfully of how well the priests of Sekhmet understood embalming cats.'

'You see?' said Thamar to Reuben; who saw nothing except that Shem and Japheth were approaching, with Noah a short way behind.

'My father would speak with you.' Shem came to a halt. He had said 'my father', and not 'father', Reuben noted. He felt sad about being an outsider again: someone Noah liked but disapproved of – as a plain man always disapproves of artists. *And* someone he had, in a moment's fury, cursed. Reuben stood up, outwardly calm, but watchful.

'Hrrumpth,' said Noah, also coming to a halt, and expanding his chest. It expanded easily since he had been so favoured above those wicked tribesmen who had drowned. On the front of his long robe his wife had carefully embroidered a large inaccurate dove with a leaf held in its beak. When Noah's chest went in and out the dove appeared to breathe too, and the leaf shivered. Thamar admired the effect.

'Well, Reuben – I mean, Ham – '

'Reuben will do,' said Reuben easily. 'It seems to come more naturally to you now. I've always truly preferred my own name. Borrowing a dead man's never appealed to me.' His tone said 'and such a man'.

Noah went red beneath his beard. It was like a

7

sunset behind snowy peaks. Thamar, who had never seen such a thing, admired this effect too.

'As a matter of fact, boy, I was going to address you as Canaan. Just that. Canaan. It has a good solid sound. Like something that could be built up. Yes – I like it.'

'I – see.'

'Canaan!' Thamar gave the joyous laugh that always disturbed Noah in a peculiar way. 'Am I to call you Canaan, too?'

'You want us to go there?' asked Reuben.

'No need to put it like that,' said Noah testily. 'It's not a question of wanting. We all have work to do, and I was suggesting where you might like to start yours. That is all. And there's no hurry, of course. Take your time.'

'We feel you must take your time – ' said Shem.

'As much as you like. No hurry,' added Japheth.

'We may want to hurry.' Thamar put her nose in the air. It was a pretty nose. Noah tried not to look at it. 'Just before you came we were planning to go right down into Kemi, to see if anyone was left alive. That's further than Canaan, isn't it? Much further. We can stop off on the way, and Reuben can have a good look at his inheritance.'

She began a few steps from an ancient, rhythmic dance, as though she had forgotten Noah's presence. Shem couldn't take his eyes off her, but she was only aware of Reuben. She had been trapped by a fit of temper, and now Reuben would think she had agreed to Kemi. She was right. Reuben did.

'It will be a terrible journey.' Noah was awkwardly pulling at his beard. 'Terrible. You must take your elephants and camels, of course, and they shall be loaded up with all that we can spare. You'll want Benoni?' There was a hopeful note in his voice; he had always coveted Reuben's magnificent herd dog.

'Benoni – and Benoni's mate. But if they have puppies, and we survive the journey, two shall be sent back to you one day. This is a promise.'

'You will let us have some of Meluseth's kittens?' asked Japheth eagerly. 'That is, if you don't leave for a moon or so. The mice will be getting out of hand.'

'What? I will never abandon a child.' Cefalu rose to his full arch and walked stiffly round Japheth in an insulting way. 'I have strong views on education and morals, and the way fish is eaten is most important too. The bones come out first. To eat round bones, as though you knew no better, is a common habit.'

'We shall see, we shall see,' Reuben soothed him, 'but I think you and Meluseth may have a great many children, Cefalu. To take them all on this journey may be difficult.'

'Meluseth will be upset,' argued Cefalu. 'She is feeling so fulfilled.' But a future of many kittens made him thoughtful, and he spoke no more of education.

'Talk about it with my wife.' Noah looked at Reuben. 'She has always been so fond of you.'

'Yes, she has,' murmured Shem and Japheth together jealously. They too were fond of Reuben and Thamar, but would be glad to see them go. Noah's

9

wife was given to favouritism, and they were tired of
having Reuben's chosen lamb stew seethed in dried
herbs every day.

Thamar watched Noah and his sons withdrawing
to the Ark, which still rested lopsidedly on Ararat
beside their tents. Then she put her arms round
Reuben's neck. 'You will hold me to Kemi, now?'

He looked at her anxiously. 'I would like to. Am I
taking you to too great danger?'

'No greater than in Canaan,' said Thamar generously, although she thought this was untrue.

'The worst danger would be for anyone to recognize me before we reached the King's presence. I
wonder – '

'But you've grown a beard, on the Ark. A fine
beard.' Thamar prodded it, and laughed. 'Perhaps
no one will recognize you – not even the Lord of
the Two Lands himself. Who will think of a slave
musician, when the Prince and Princess of Canaan
are announced?'

PART ONE

The King of Kemi

The Water Garden
of Ay

Not far from the Palace of White Walls, down in
Kemi, was an opulent house belonging to the Court
Chamberlain Ay. It was built in the new style, with
airy latticed windows, and there were many gay-
coloured hangings which could be lowered to keep
out wind or flying sand. The rooms were frescoed by
cunning artists, who painted exquisite green marsh
grasses, and fish gliding among lotus roots, and wea-
sels stealthy and bright-eyed stalking stiff, upright
hares. It was a new house because Ay was a provincial who had lately gained his high position. Now
he kept his own bird-catchers and weavers and
beekeepers, as well as gardeners and servants and
many slaves. Yet he was greatly scorned at court,
where the King's way of raising men to high office
because they deserved it was a modern habit
frowned on by the hereditary officers of state.

They sniffed at Ay's provincial manners, at his
bluntness, his curious belief in honesty. It was fortu-
nate they were beneath the young King's thumb – he
was already a great man, as Reuben had prophesied –
or they would have poisoned Ay. As it was they

13

confined themselves to sniffing, although they would not have sniffed if they had seen his daughter. She was very young, and had never been to court.

Meri-Mekhmet was as lovely and graceful as her mother had been, and inherited nothing from her father but his stubborn, uncomfortable honesty. Young men in the provinces, attracted by her beauty as bees to honey, and even more attracted by her father's growing wealth, had sometimes withdrawn discomfited by the honey's flavour: those cool summing-up brown eyes between long dark lashes seemed to see right into their mean little thoughts which were full of greed and lazy desire for an easy, nursed life. So, at the age of sixteen, Meri-Mekhmet devoted her life to music, to her gardens, to her kind, dull, honest father; and thought sadly it would be pointless making scenes in order to visit that corrupt court from which her father carefully kept her, if all the young men were as weak, soft and contemptible as those she already knew. Sometimes her father worried about this, though not often. If he had a fault it was a selfish need to keep his daughter to himself: she was so sympathetic, played the harp and flute so well, and reminded him constantly of his dead wife.

Every now and then he would say: 'I must arrange about your life, my daughter.'

And she would reply: 'Not yet, my father – not unless you know a man different from those I have already seen!'

Then Ay would shake his head, and admit that the

14

courtiers were rich and handsome – but they struck cold horror to his heart; and he would add there was only one man he admired in the whole capital city of Men-nofer: the King himself.

At this point Meri-Mekhmet usually gave a delicate sniff through her delicate nostrils. She had never seen the King, except as a far distant blur of grandeur in the Temple of Ptah on great feast days; and she was sure her father was biased in his favour. She thought poorly of a man who from tradition kept a Great Royal Wife as well as a harem, and had been unable, since his accession some sixty-eight moons ago, to make a clean sweep of his court's corruption. She was very young.

Ay was scandalized by her views, and said so. He had loved her mother and nobody else, but that was beside the point. Most people in that age would have thought him disgracefully odd. The King had acted traditionally, and was in favour with the gods. Besides, he was known to be a god himself, and the son of the sun. It was disrespectful to sniff. He said so; and hoped Meri-Mekhmet wasn't growing eccentric – 'like your Aunt Tut'.

'Then I might also be a priestess of Hathor,' said Meri-Mekhmet serenely. She raised one hand and shook it in the air, as though rattling a sistrum before a goddess.

'You would be lucky if they accepted you. And besides – ' He looked up sharply. One of his servants had entered, bowing.

'For the ears of Ay alone.'

Ay made a gesture with his hand, but already Meri-Mekhmet was moving away. These interruptions were a part of life since her father's court appointment, and were often surrounded by silly secrecy. Afterwards he would tell her what they were about, and would discuss his problems with her, since she had good brains – too good for a woman, he would add, sighing, as he thought over her excellent, gently given advice.

Today she walked absently into the outer court-yard before the house, and stopped in some confusion. She had forgotten that official callers for her father would bring a retinue. The courtyard was full of young men, talking to each other in affected voices. A simple gilded litter was drawn up near the entrance. Silence fell as the young men realized her presence. The courtyard seemed to be all eyes – brazenly considering eyes. There was a general move towards her. Meri-Mekhmet drew her linen scarf about her face, and retreated into the shadow of the house with her graceful swaying walk – not before overhearing words she was meant to hear.

'Beasts!' she told herself angrily, as she made her way to her favourite water garden. 'Court baboons – ' and then hoped the Great White One was not offended. (He was also a baboon, but sacred.)

The garden was calming. Meri-Mekhmet sat down beside an ornamental pool where red fish swam to and fro, and felt her annoyance subside. It was so peaceful here. A light boat of papyrus reeds rocked on the water. Butterflies skimmed over it and settled

16

like jewels on water-lilies and lotus flowers. There was silence except for the sound of fountains, a faint whisper of reeds, and the small, sudden plop when a red fish rose to an unwary insect. A kingfisher flickered like a blue flame above the reflection of a willow. Meri-Mekhmet watched him happily.

I'll be a priestess of Hathor, she thought. She took off her sandals – usually she went barefoot – and dabbled her toes in the water so that the red fish had hysterics and swam away. She laughed, and drew her feet back on to dry land. She sat curled up in the sun on the hot stone, and went into a pleasurable midday trance while time slipped by unnoticed, and the sun slipped a little sideways in the sky.

She woke from dreaming when a breeze started to blow. It was refreshing, after midday heat. She glanced sideways along the path, saw an unexpected shadow there, glanced upwards, and found herself in company. A young man stood watching her. He wore a plain wide gold necklet, a kilt, and plaited, gilded sandals such as her father wore. He looked full of silent amazement, and might have never seen a girl before. She noticed he was very awkward, for when she rose he made no move towards her, and was speechless. He simply stood there, very upright. He was no courtier, or he would have known how to behave. She felt sorry for him in his awkwardness, and kindly towards him. Was it possible he was one of those brash young men who had lounged in her father's outer courtyard? She thought not.

They stood there face to face till she began to

laugh. It was so funny, somehow. At first he looked surprised, and then he laughed too, sympathetically, as though he found her reaction unexpected but amusing.

'Oh, but I'm sorry!' she said at last, between gasps, and holding her sides in a way that would have shocked her father. 'It's easy to see you've never been to court, praise be to Hathor! You're not at all like the young men who come to see my father and scrape, and speak in honeyed voices, and look so – so . . .' Her voice trailed away. She couldn't describe the annoying way they looked. 'I've never been to court, either' (she must try to put him at ease, now they had both stopped laughing), 'so you needn't think I was laughing at you for – Shall we sit in the sun? It's lovely here. And the fish are calming, not nearly so difficult as people.'

'How thoughtful of them.' The young man came a little closer. She gestured towards a patch of stone by the pool, where a soft green creeping plant made a suitable cushion, and he handed her to it with a self-possession that made her wonder if he *had* been to court, after all. Then he knelt beside her, bent forward, and dabbled his fingers thoughtfully in the water. There was a look of self-mocking amusement on his face, if she could have seen it.

'You – you weren't out there with those young men who – who were rude to me in the outer court-yard? Were you?' she asked doubtfully.

He brought his glance back to her face. 'They were

rude – to you?' There was such anger behind the words that she was startled.

She bit her lip. 'You know what they are like.'

'By Set, they shall learn their place!' he said between his teeth. 'I will teach them it.'

Again she started to laugh. 'Oh, please forgive me, but each of those wretched striplings is almost as powerful as my father! They would have a knife stuck in your ribs without a thought! But thank you for being cross – that was friendly. Could you tell me – was anyone still with my father when you came through the house?'

'He was quite alone.'

She was curious. 'It's unlike him not to come with visitors himself . . .'

The young man smiled. She thought him plain, but he had a very engaging smile. It lent distinction to his face, which it otherwise lacked, except for a pair of eyes as noticeable as her own.

'I had heard of your father's gardens. He gave me the privilege of walking here alone. I had something on my mind, and wished to think about it.'

'I'm disturbing you? Shall I go?'

'Please stay.' He put a hand on her arm to draw her back. She sat down again, and looked at him under her lashes. Who was this odd young man, who felt a need to walk alone in an elderly Chamberlain's gardens? He must be a solitary person, like herself.

'What are you thinking of so deeply?'

'I'm wondering who you are.' There was a question in her voice, and a slight note of reproof.

He bit his lip, as though vexed at something. 'I have several names, but my mother always called me Merenkere.'

'Why, it's a little like my own: Meri-Mekhmet. But no – you cannot be called that.' She shook her head. 'It's utterly absurd. You are joking: that's the King's name, and no man shares the King's name. You will be eaten by a crocodile, if you make jokes like that.'

'You fear this King would be ready with his crocodiles? But it is not a joke,' he insisted gravely. 'I was given the King's name at birth. My mother was high in favour at the court. There was nothing she could not do – or have done.'

She looked at him gravely. She didn't want to believe he was a liar, yet she could not think he was brought up at court.

'You don't wish to tell me your real name? Then I'll call you what you like – but not in public, or it may bring you harm. Why do you want to take the King's name anyway? Do you admire him so?'

'I am the King's man,' he admitted shortly. 'Whether I like it or not.'

Meri-Mekhmet gave the tiny sniff that so annoyed her father.

'You at least do not approve of him?' Merenkere gave her his disarming smile.

'I'm afraid he must be absolutely disgusting,' she said; and added, in sudden panic, 'You won't tell anyone I said so? It would be dangerous for my father.' How did she know he could be trusted? She felt he could but –

20

'*Absolutely* disgusting?'

'Please,' she poked at his bare arm with a desperate finger. 'Promise.'

'Of course, if he's absolutely disgusting, he might have your father killed, mightn't he?' he said with a faint smile.

'Oh, do stop joking, sir – it is – '

'Merenkere.'

'Merenkere, then – you must promise.'

He took her hand and held it comfortingly. 'I promise – on one condition. Now you tell me why the King is absolutely disgusting. Did your father tell you so?'

'Isis and Osiris, no! My father adores the King. He thinks everything he does is wonderful.' She sighed. 'In some ways I'm afraid my father is a very simple man.' She shook her head. 'Not at all used to kings.'

'Very few people are, really. Least of all the kings themselves. You feel you would have seen through this one at once?'

'Well, if he's so wonderful, why can't he stop his courtiers being cor – corrupt, to start with?'

'Why, indeed?'

'And then the man must be a monster – he has hundreds of foreign princesses in his harem.'

'Ninety-three,' said the King automatically.

'Ugh! That makes him worse. There's something so deliberate about ninety-three. Don't you think it's disgusting?'

The King said he did. He hadn't thought so before,

THE WATER GARDEN OF AY

but now he felt like a small boy who has overeaten himself and suddenly feels sick.

'My father says it's just tradition. But you're more like me, you're all right,' said Meri-Mekhmet happily, and gave him her sudden smile, which made the King blink as though he was staring at the sun.

They looked at each other gravely. Then: 'Great Osiris!' said the King in an unsteady voice, and took her hand and kissed it. He rose to his feet, said: 'I – your father will be waiting for me. I'll come again', and strode away towards the house.

Meri-Mekhmet looked after him in amazement. She had a curious feeling in her mind, quite unaccounted for, and it was not to do with priestesses or temples.

'Of course, he's a terrible country bumpkin,' she told the fish, 'almost as simple as a peasant. But there's something truly genuine about him. After all, we were provincials ourselves, till father came to court.'

A Court Chamberlain's
Quandary

Meri-Mekhmet's father had taken to flapping round
his house and making odd noises of distress like a
pintail duck disturbed by careless hunters. He would
gobble with a red face in a way which thoroughly
alarmed his daughter but made little sense: except
that he wished her back in the country; and, since it
was the first time Meri-Mekhmet hadn't wished it for
herself, she merely made soothing noises, wondered
if she ought to call in the court physicians with their
charms and incense burners, and tried to distract her
father's mind by talking of the pleasant, plain young
man who came to see her nearly every day.

'Do not talk about it, daughter, I beg you,' said
poor Ay, who had been sworn to secrecy by his King,
and flattened, when he mildly protested, by a flash
from the King's remarkable eyes. Did he dare take
his daughter to the country, he wondered, and leave
her there? How angry would the King be if he did?
Very angry, he answered himself. Yes, said the first
part of Ay, but the King is a great man, and a good
man, and fair-minded. He is also a young man, said
the second part of Ay, and in love; and young men

in love are impetuous, though not many young men
in love are gods and have the free gift of royal crocodiles. So Ay bothered and dithered, and failed to
put it to the touch, and countered Meri-Mekhmet's
artless confidences with talk of Aunt Tut and the
Temple of Hathor. He had always said that no good
would come of the King's slipping out to visit his
officials privately whenever he felt like it: a scandal-
ous new habit, and an impious, unwise one. The
gods would certainly be worried by it, although not
half so worried as the poor unhappy Court Chamberlain Ay.

'Don't you like Merenkere, Father?' asked Meri-
Mekhmet often. 'He's just the sort of quiet, pleasant
young man you always like.'

Ay ground his teeth. 'Why should I not like him?'
he growled.

'But you don't exactly seem happy when he's
here.'

'For a serious young man – and you tell me he is
serious – he does not seem to have enough to do.'

Meri-Mekhmet repeated her father's words to the
King, when they were playing draughts by the pool;
he was much amused.

'I don't see it's a funny remark. What have you
done, so to displease my father?'

'I hardly like to think,' said the King. 'I always
hoped he had feelings of affection for me.'

'Well, I'm afraid he hasn't. You must try to win
him round.'

'How may I do that?' asked the King, laughing again.

'Be nice to him.'

'I'm always nice to him.'

'Hang on his words a little – you know. Men of his age like that.'

'I'm always hanging on his words.' Merenkere took one of her pieces, and crowned a king. 'Much more often than you'd believe, Meri-Mekhmet, my first sister.'

In Kemi the words 'first sister' meant 'darling' or 'beloved'. Meri-Mekhmet went a little pink, and spoke rather fast. 'I am worried in case something is wrong with – with his mind,' she whispered. 'He does nothing but talk about crocodiles. He is obsessed by crocodiles. Don't you find it most peculiar? Should I not send for some physicians?'

'It is probably the heat,' said the King gravely. 'No – don't frighten your father by sending for physicians. Let me talk to him about these crocodiles. I have calm views on crocodiles that I'm sure to make him share.'

'You're so kind.' Meri-Mekhmet shifted a little nearer, and felt very much like a first sister. 'I can't think why he's – difficult, about you.'

The King looked at her ingenuous face and felt a bit mean. Ay was ingenuous too, and he found himself wondering if even a god-king should treat his Court Chamberlain as he was doing. Then, still looking at Meri-Mekhmet, he felt he had no choice. Not as things were. Lonely as he was on the throne, he couldn't do without his visits to the water garden. If there were not already a Great Royal Wife –

He sighed heavily, fingering an ivory piece.

'What is the matter, Merenkere?'

'Life is such a trap.'

'Is it?' She stared at him, puzzled. He forced a smile.

'Let us talk of something else. Look – you have lost the game. And I don't want to make you sad. Where is your father now?'

'I thought he was going out to see the King. But he hasn't gone, I can't think why. I'll tell you something very amusing, to cheer you up. When my father sees the King, and the King asks him his opinions, my father often tells him what *I* think! And the King believes it's his Court Chamberlain! He would never, never listen if he thought it was just me, would he? Don't you think it funny?' She laughed merrily, and looked exactly like a child, or so the King thought.

'Much funnier than you think.'

'Now you're being rude to me!' She was a little offended, and stood up as though to walk away. He pulled her down again.

'I was not. What can I give you, to make up?'

'Nothing.' She looked as suspicious as a quarrelling child. He put out a hand to touch her long black hair.

'Something to wear in all this ridiculous stuff?' He gave it a pull, as though he were another child, and they were on good terms again.

When he next came he brought with him a twisted

head-dress made of delicate gold wire set with flow-ers of turquoise and carnelian, all held together by gold cross-pieces.

Meri-Mekhmet was overawed by its beauty. 'Oh, you shouldn't have - It's beautiful – My father will never let me keep it.'

'I have already asked him, and he didn't mind.' (Well, not much, added the King to himself.)

'He must like you more than he did.'

'I hope he does not like me less. Try it on.'

He put the crown of twisted gold and jewels on her head. They stood side by side staring down at her reflection in the pool. A red fish swam across it, and spoilt the spell.

'Now you're like a princess of the royal house.'

'That I will never be!'

'Hush, it's unlucky to say such things.'

'Why unlucky? Is it such luck to be a princess – and married to a monster with ninety-three other princesses to his hand?'

'Perhaps he would get rid of his ninety-three prin-cesses, if he could marry you,' said the King desperately.

'Poor monster – and poor ninety-three princesses. Why should they suffer?'

'I do not think they would. They are not real. They are a tradition.'

'Even a tradition might have feelings. Now you're talking as the King probably thinks of them. And that is why I say he is a monster, don't you see?'

'This poor monster! I have a fellow feeling for him,

anyway.' He gave a sad smile. 'Do you not like my gift?'

'So long as I don't have to remind you of a princess, then I love it.'

'Will you kiss me for it, Meri-Mekhmet?'

She did.

The next time Merenkere came to see Meri-Mekhmet, she told him her father was ill in bed.

'So they told – It's not worry about those crocodiles, I hope?' asked the King guiltily. 'I thought his mind was soothed.'

'Oh, you were wonderful with him. No, I think he needs country air. He says that little crown you gave me makes him think all the time of the small house he was born in, but I can't quite follow the connection. I'm afraid he must be very ill. My Aunt Tut, who is a priestess of Hathor and formidable, has come to stay, and be with me.'

The King looked round him nervously. He knew Aunt Tut well, and feared she might say something stupid. Meri-Mekhmet reassured him: 'Oh, she is not so formidable that you need fear her.'

'I do not,' said the King untruthfully.

'Anyway, she's with my father, dosing him with a syrup of figs and dung-beetles in honey. It will take some time, because he will not swallow it. Merenkere, you're looking very worried today. Shall I send for our singers, to amuse you?'

'Ah no – it's nothing. It is just I had some news which has upset me.'

'Tell me.'

'I had once a great friend, a remarkable musician. He was the King's musician, in fact. I've just heard that an unusual flood has covered all the land where he was living – he and his wife must be dead.' The King sighed. 'Poor Reuben.'

'How sad.' Meri-Mekhmet's eyes filled with tears. 'But perhaps they escaped.'

'I'm afraid they are dead these many moons. Word travels slowly from that country. The flood has ebbed, but no one brings me news of Reuben and his wife.'

'But how came this news of the flood?'

'One of my – ' The King checked himself. 'It's rumoured round Men-nofer,' he said more carefully, 'that a Prince and Princess of Canaan have arrived in the city, and are staying at some humble hostelry or other. Staying – and starving. Poor things, they arrived with scarcely any belongings but some eleph-ants and camels and such. I'm afraid they've been very hard hit. I must – I mean, they are bound to be received at court.'

'Then news may get back to you of your Reuben,' said Meri-Mekhmet, 'although you may have to wait for it. Let me fetch my harp and play for you.' She jumped up. 'The harp is lovely out here – when one accompanies it by singing.'

'Your voice is always lovely, anyway – ' but the King held her firmly back. 'Look – there's a king-fisher! I have a feeling he will bring us luck. His shadow flits between ours as though he would bind them both together.'

'The priests say our shadows are a special piece of our own selves,' said Meri-Mekhmet.

'Perhaps they're right. I wish I could leave my shadow here with yours.'

The Lord of Diadems

The Court Chamberlain Ay was sleeping so heavily that Aunt Tut had to explain the matter to her anxious niece.

'With the dung-beetles and figs there was mingled a draught most potently calming to the nerves. For a day and a night your father will be as one dead, and then will wake restored to health.'

'It will not harm him?' asked poor Meri-Mekhmet.

'Harm him?' Tut bristled; she had reached an age and ugliness when all her vanity was concerned with her important office, and her cleverness. 'My child, I overlook your remark simply because of your silliness and youth.'

'I am very sorry, my father's sister.'

'No matter at all.' She graciously took the ripest fig from a dish, and handed a small unripe one to Meri-Mekhmet. 'In fact your father's sleep is a very good thing, for it gives me time to make arrangements for your life.'

Meri-Mekhmet put back the fig.

'But my father himself – '

'Your father, my sistrum! Tell me: what exact

arrangements has your father made about your future? And tell me nothing vague for I know he could be vague for five hundred moons and nothing come of it.'

'Well, he – ' Meri-Mekhmet stopped.

'Yes?' pounced Tut, triumphantly.

'He – he does not like me to go to court, so – '

'Hathor – may she be venerated for love's sake! – what idiocy! Why not?'

'He – he finds the courtiers corrupt.'

'Ha!' Tut gobbled as her brother did, when he was upset. 'A new discovery indeed. And one which would lead to total celibacy if the fathers of all daughters paid attention to it. So your father hasn't arranged your marriage. Where else is he looking? To the Temples?'

Meri-Mekhmet was silent.

'Hathor,' said Tut knowledgeably. 'I thought so. In other words, to me. Well, that's all right, and I'm the last person not to do what I may for a close relation. All the same, you can be married and a priestess of Hathor, as you know. And I don't think we should rule out marriage, yet. There must be some young man, somewhere, your father would approve – it's all his laziness – ' She stopped, and eyed her niece sharply. 'I see. There is someone your father does *not* approve?'

'I can't see why he doesn't approve of him.' Poor Meri-Mekhmet twisted her fingers in and out round each other as though they were the gold wires in her coronet.

'Has he no wealth?'

'Yes – no – I don't know. He is shabby, sometimes. But he brought me a beautiful present.'

'There is something dark, of Set's world, about this,' said the shrewd old priestess, and the sinews of her neck wriggled like snakes as she shook her head. 'I suppose your father – Sekhmet watch over him, he was always a fool! – has asked no questions to any purpose. This young man has made no formal offer for you?'

'I – I do not think so.' Meri-Mekhmet, who had been trying to fend off doubts and worries for some time, burst into tears.

'Be quiet, child. We shall get nowhere if you make such noise. Most things in life can be worked out like arithmetic, so long as noise is avoided. How often have you seen this young man? Once? Twice? Many times?'

'Oh many, many,' wept Meri-Mekhmet. 'He comes almost every day.'

Tut rose to her feet with a furious jangle of bracelets. 'High time I appeared on the scene! This must not be allowed. Who is this young man?'

Meri-Mekhmet was about to tell her, when she recalled her promise of not repeating Merenkere's name.

'Please, my father's sister, do not make me say.'

'I must know it.'

Meri-Mekhmet cast round in her mind, and came up with 'Merenkeret.'

Tut searched her own mind. 'Familiar – and yet

33

not entirely – But what springs to mind at once, child, is that this young man is already married and has a most jealous wife.'

'Oh no.' Meri-Mekhmet stared at her in horror. 'I know he – That is, he wouldn't – he would have told me.'

Tut snorted. A snort full of meaning and forty years' disillusionment. 'When is he coming to see you again?'

'He – he never says. He just comes. I expect he will come today.'

'As I thought. He has to creep out when he can. This time he will have me to reckon with, my dear child. When Merenkeret comes, you shall bring him straight to me.'

At midday Meri-Mekhmet went out into the water garden lonely and afraid, and waited for Merenkere to come. She picked the garden cornflowers, and wondered where the kingfisher had gone. She waited a long, long time, while Aunt Tut gathered her dragon forces together in a powerful snooze. But the sun god moved majestically across the sky towards his nightly journey through the underworld; and Merenkere never came.

'Well, your young man loiters, child.'

'He loves me, I know he does,' said Meri-Mekhmet defiantly.

'Of course he loves you, he is plainly not a simpleton. I am not questioning his love, only his behaviour. This is a melancholy subject. Let us change it.

My priestesses have sent word that tonight the King gives special audience to some trumpery Prince and Princess from the north. Since it's my right in Hathor to be there I shall attend, and take you with me, while your ridiculous father sleeps. How does that appeal to you? We'll have a close look at these corrupt courtiers together, and you will learn they are ordinary people, though a little spoilt.'

'My father would hate me to do this!'

'Of course he would, which teaches us all the blessings of sleep - may Set be praised for sleep and night,' said the old priestess piously. 'Did he tell you to obey me, child, while I was here?'

'Yes,' said Meri-Mekhmet honestly but reluctantly, 'he did.'

'Then have your attendants look out your finest clothes, and let me see your ornaments before you choose them. I will order the litters.' The large, slightly bloodshot eyes in the haggard face considered the young girl. 'We will have you beautiful, but not so beautiful that you attract the King. I myself would not be against it, even for a god he is a most delightful man, but he has already a Great Royal Wife – sickly creature! – and I do not think your father would approve.'

'Oh, nor would I,' said Meri-Mekhmet fervently.

The daughter of Ay was very nervous as they approached the Palace of White Walls, but she had been well trained by her dead mother, and showed no signs of strain, except for rather hurried breathing;

and she had to admit her first visit to a great king's court was exciting. So exciting that at first she hardly noticed anything about her, as they walked through the outer courts, conducted by a slave. Aunt Tut was very much at home, greeted here and greeted there; and this gave her niece some comfort and confidence, and helped her bear the sensation of being pierced by innumerable eyes.

Although her father had often described the grandeur of the King's court she was unprepared for the atmosphere of high-pitched solemnity, the sense of religious ecstacy which was the keynote of contact between subjects and King. Her father, after all, talked of his master as a highly intelligent young man, of great personality: an absolute ruler, and a good one. But he hadn't emphasized that this King was also the High Priest of the Two Lands, the Horus of Gold, the Son of Re; nor described the awe people felt when they found themselves nearing the room where the living incarnation of a god was crowned and throned.

As Tut and Meri-Mekhmet approached they heard the scattered notes of silver trumpets, and looking down a wide corridor saw a distant procession form itself.

'The Prince and Princess of Canaan, already!' hissed Tut, and charged towards the hangings that hid the audience room from their gaze. Two officers of the King's Guard, standing with crossed spears, lowered their weapons and drew back the hangings in one accustomed movement. Meri-Mekhmet followed her aunt into the Presence, and immediately they prostrated themselves in the first of the prescribed obeisances to the Sovereign.

When they rose she was dazzled by her surroundings, and walked behind Tut in a daze, copying her movements, and at intervals sinking to the ground. The room was long and wide, its pillars exquisitely painted. Everywhere were the symbols of bee, plant, vulture and serpent. There was gold and a great deal of silver, for in Kemi silver was more valuable than gold. The general effect was gorgeous, particularly where round the King were grouped his fan bearers, his great officers of state, his chamberlains, his Vizier, his High Priests and his Great Royal Wife. All this Meri-Mekhmet barely took in as they approached. Her scornful feelings towards a King who had ninety-three foreign princesses in his harem, *and* a Great Royal Wife, crumbled. In the face of such splendour she felt her criticisms had been those of a little girl. She had been totally unprepared for the atmosphere in this audience room. She walked meekly behind her aunt with eyes downcast as etiquette demanded, until they stood at the throne's foot. There they knelt, and bowed their foreheads to the floor.

Merenkere sat wearily enthroned, still as a statue. Long and arduous training had taught him the rigidity of a carved symbol. Ritual and purification and still more ritual overshadowed his life. He was a man in the shell of a god, or a god in the shell of a man. His eyes stared impersonally from his head towards the entrance, where the trumpeters had taken up a stand to announce the coming Prince and Princess. Although he had not lowered his eyes, nor allowed recognition into his face, he had recognized Tut when she entered; but the girl who followed her he didn't notice, for he was accustomed to the retinues of priests and priestesses who followed their superiors about the court. A young girl with black hair, in a fine pleated linen dress, was normal company for a woman of Tut's position in the Temple of Hathor.

Now Tut rose ungracefully to her feet, and Meri-Mekhmet stood up after her. The Great Royal Wife, who sat on a smaller throne to the King's left, stared petulantly at such beauty, and wished she had it. The King lowered his weary gaze for one second – and gave a violent start.

The small movement, after such perfect rigidity, was, to anyone facing him, excessive. Tut blinked her amazement. Even Meri-Mekhmet in her young confusion realized something had surprised the great god, the monster, and defied everything her aunt had told her of custom and religious training, and raised her enormous eyes, and looked.

She saw for the first time all the glory of the royal house. The King wore the Nemes head-dress of striped blue and gold which framed his face in its stiff folds. An enamelled cobra raised its head above his forehead. He wore a simple white kilt and gold sandals, but his jewelled necklet was wide to his shoulders, and deep, shaped like the rays of the sun, and his heavy bracelets and anklets were studded with turquoise, carnelian and lapis. He sat on leopard skins, and wore the symbolic lion's tail and false beard of office, and in his hand he held the ruler's crook and flail.

Meri-Mekhmet stared at the High Priest, the god, Lord of Diadems and of the Two Lands, the man she had called a monster; and the monster's face was the face of her unassuming Merenkere.

The King saw her mouth open, and her face whiten. His own lips had paled with horror, and the crossed hands holding crook and flail shook imperceptibly. His eyes held Meri-Mekhmet's for a moment, and into them he tried desperately to put love, and explanation, and a plea for understanding; and naturally failed. The raw simplicity of his emotion was not enough.

Meri-Mekhmet wanted to scream, to run. She was almost blinded by the truth's dreadful clarity. Her Aunt Tut thought – much annoyed after her schooling – that her niece had mistaken the number of necessary prostrations: but in fact Meri-Mekhmet had fallen on her face because her knees refused to hold her up; and she stayed there, although her aunt's foot prodded her, and her aunt's lips hissed agonized instructions sideways. It took a small gesture from the Great Royal Wife, and resulting help from a fan bearer, to get her to her feet. She didn't look at Merenkere again as she followed Tut to one side of the room, where the courtiers parted to let them through. Her behaviour had caused sympathy and gratification. It was not unusual for people to be affected in the god's presence, some had even died.

And it was generally felt that Meri-Mekhmet's beauty would excuse everything except a scream.

Tut, however, was not so amiable. 'I have never been so humbled in my life,' she hissed at her dazed and trembling niece. 'Your father should have kept you in the country amongst slaves and peasants, stupid girl. Are we a family to faint before royalty?' And she borrowed a fan and fanned Meri-Mekhmet in a disowning way. Luckily at that moment the silver trumpets produced a positive cascade of notes and everyone's attention was taken by the Prince and Princess of Canaan's entry, and open interest was roused in their outlandish dress.

'Hathor be praised,' muttered Tut, fanning less fluently, 'no one will think of your behaviour, girl, when they look at this.' In fact, Thamar's obeisances – which Reuben had taught her – though unusual were astonishingly graceful, and caught the Vizier Senusmet's eye quite dangerously. This may have been as well, since it gave him no time to recognize Reuben in a beard.

The poor young King Merenkere did recognize his former musician, however, and for someone who had received two shocks in rapid succession remained astoundingly composed. He controlled his shaking hands, but could not restrain himself from giving one desperate glance into the crowd where Meri-Mekhmet had vanished. Then he resumed his royal, immobile stance. To look at him no one could have believed his mind was in agony, his one desire to leap from his throne and follow Meri-Mekhmet's quick escape; for, as soon as Tut's attention was really held by Reuben's and Thamar's procession up the room, she had slipped quietly between the courtiers towards a small side entrance, and disappeared beyond it.

Two Encounters

In the Palace gardens it was dark. Meri-Mekhmet blundered into them thankfully, confused by the numbers of rooms and corridors through which she had run. All she really wanted, unknowingly, was to escape from herself – the self holding in its mind's eye the picture of Merenkere on his throne, beside him his unnoticeable but intolerably present Great Royal Wife.

The gardens were warm, and scented. Meri-Mekhmet was only glad of their darkness. She stumbled down a path between sweet-smelling bushy plants towards a tinkling sound and rustle of reeds which suggested a water garden; and since this too clearly reminded her of all that was now smashed to pieces, she swerved to her left where the shadow of a tamarisk offered shelter. Here she sank to the ground and put her arms around her knees, her head down on them. She started to cry – large, hopeless tears which flowed as though they would never stop. Near at hand a waterbird croaked a warning to its mate. Meri-Mekhmet felt utterly alone under the warm blue-velvet sky.

In the audience room Tut soon missed her niece and made discreet inquiries, but no one had seen her go. It was unlikely harm would come to Meri-Mekhmet in the royal Palace, but the priestess was furiously annoyed and made a mental note to wash her hands of a girl so lost to custom and gratitude. When the court at last prostrated itself and the King withdrew she mentioned the matter to the Court Chamberlain on duty that night, and then stalked off to sit and work herself into a fret, while the Palace slaves searched for the missing girl. At last she fell asleep, her mouth open and small snorts coming through her nose. A fan bearer took up station close by, and no one disturbed the venerated priestess of Hathor although she was very much in everyone's way.

Meanwhile, Thamar was being fed with sweet wine, cakes and fruit in a little ante-room, and Reuben was closeted with the King. Merenkere greeted him with honest pleasure, but it was subdued, and his general manner was so unhappy that Reuben, in his usual open way, dared to ask him what was wrong.

'We should not have come, my lord the King?' he asked anxiously. 'It was lacking in respect to get ourselves into the Sovereign's presence as we did, but your servant feared what would happen to his wife if the Vizier or High Priest of Sekhmet, or even Kenamut, intercepted us before we could claim protection. If we have offended my Sovereign, my lord – '

'No, Reuben, no,' said the King absently, 'it was a good joke – and one to make my worthy Vizier gnash what remains of his teeth when he realizes it – but do not make one like it every day.' (Reuben reddened at the mild rebuke.) 'As for Kenamut, you needn't fear him: he has disappeared. They say he offended some Nile deity – which is another way of saying he had enemies. Even here in Men-nofer it's unsafe to be too vile. Sekhmet's High Priest lies ill in his bed, babbling all day to his goddess words no one can understand, although held to be of great importance to the Two Lands. I myself think them the ravings of a sick old man who dropped like a stone on the Treasury floor one day, and has neither walked nor used his right arm since. This opinion, I need hardly say, is for your ears alone.'

He sighed, and sat down miserably on a couch. Reuben continued to stand, until after some while the King started as though he had forgotten all about his presence there, and motioned him to sit upon a rug.

'That beard!' Merenkere smiled faintly. 'It makes you look like an uncouth Syrian! My Majesty's astute Vizier will not be deceived too long – you had best remove it before you grow conspicuous. I have a court jeweller with a beard', and here he suddenly looked more amused, 'but one such atrocity is enough.' He gave Reuben a piercing glance. 'Have you returned here to resume your duties as my slave?'

For answer, Reuben drew off and held out to him

the ring Merenkere had given him as token of freedom in the Temple of Ptah. 'If my Sovereign, my
lord desires his ring again,' he said without a tremor,
'it is here.'

The King took it in his hand, and twisted it round
and round between his fingers. Then he returned it.

'I freed you, Reuben. The King does not go back on
his word. Will you stay here as my court musician?'

'It was what I hoped for, my lord the King,' said
Reuben frankly, 'if I may return sometimes to visit
my inheritance in the north – for Canaan has been
granted me.'

The King raised his eyebrows. 'It must be a muddy
inheritance since that flood; but by all means go
when you will, my musician. Permission is granted
– so long as you return.'

'I shall always return, your Majesty – there was
no greater pleasure than playing before my lord the
King.'

Merenkere nodded, unsmilingly. His melancholy
had returned. He clapped his hands, and one of his
body servants entered and prostrated himself.

'Hemi, do you recognize this man?'

'It is, my Sovereign, my lord's missing musician.'

'You have better sight than my Majesty's noble
Vizier,' said the King, who put much trust in Hemi's
discretion. 'My former slave Reuben is now my court
musician, as well as being Prince of some land
entirely covered in mud. Take him to the apartments
prepared for him and his wife, and see no one knows

the truth till I myself have informed the Vizier Senusmet.'

'It is done, O Sovereign, my lord.'

'I am so greatly in your Majesty's debt.' Reuben knelt before the King, took his hand, and bowed his forehead on it.

'Your return is very welcome to me,' said Merenkere, 'never more so than now.' He looked over Reuben's bowed head. 'Hemi, you have something on your mind.'

'My Sovereign, my lord is as usual all-seeing,' replied the servant. 'There is a little trouble in the Palace. A young girl is missing.'

'Well, look for her,' said the King, bored.

'O Sovereign, my lord, we have looked high and low, and the Court Chamberlain Ket's temper is near to bursting. The venerable priestess of Hathor, Tut, will not go to her brother's house until her niece is found.'

The King went even paler than he was already. Reuben, raising his head, was surprised at the expression on his face; was surprised to hear a stutter in the King's voice when he said; 'It – it is M-Meri-Mekhmet, the Court Chamberlain Ay's d-daughter, who is missing?'

'O Sovereign, my lord, I do not know her name, but she came with the venerable priestess to the audience, and ran from the room while no one noticed her.'

The King rose to his feet in agitation, almost upsetting Reuben as he did so. 'Find her! Find her at once

– no one is to cease looking till every corner of the Palace has been searched, and every corner of the gardens. And when you have found her do not take her to the priestess, but bring her here to me.' He turned away, and Reuben heard him murmur, 'Osiris, that she has not run out into Men-nofer, at night, alone!'

The servant hesitated, and Reuben hesitated, seeing the King was so upset. But Merenkere said harshly, 'Go. And you too, Reuben. Let no one come near my Majesty again, until they bring me news of Meri-Mekhmet's whereabouts.'

A young officer of the King's Guard found Meri-Mekhmet by the tamarisk. At first he was pleased, and then dismayed, for he had never known anyone before who point-blank refused the King's command.

'It is the Sovereign's order,' he said unbelievingly.

'I do not care what the Sovereign orders.' Meri-Mekhmet's lips quivered. 'You may take me to the priestess Tut, if she is still here.'

But the soldier knew his duty. 'If you will not come, daughter of Ay,' he said reprovingly, 'I shall have to carry you.'

Meri-Mekhmet turned to run, but her sandal caught on a tree root, which gave the soldier time to seize her. He called one of his comrades and between them they managed to carry her to the Palace, not without difficulty. In the end they were fairly rough, for she fought and kicked and bit and struggled and with her nails did much damage here and there. Such a thing had never been seen before in Men-nofer, where women almost died of pleasure if the King looked their way. One of the young men suggested they should drown her in the pond, rather than take her to the King's presence where she might do him harm.

'No,' replied the other, removing his chin from Meri-Mekhmet's thumbnail, 'for if our lord the King came to hear of it – ' and didn't complete his sentence. But when at last they hauled Meri-Mekhmet before Merenkere they took good care to hold her till they saw what she would do.

She kept her eyes stubbornly downcast. The King's voice said, with faint unhappy amusement in it, 'Child, what damage you have done my faithful guard!' And then, 'Let her go.'

'O Sovereign, my lord – ' One soldier hesitantly gripped her arm, but at the look on his Sovereign's face he dropped his hand, and scuttled backward from the Presence with his comrade. Outside, he said: 'Well, he's thought to be a very strong god, let us hope that he can manage her.'

Very slowly and deliberately Meri-Mekhmet prostrated herself on the floor. It was the attitude of submission, but she managed to make it one of scorn, and Merenkere felt himself lose height.

'You mustn't do that,' he said in a shaken voice.

'If I have done it wrong, O Sovereign, my lord,' said Meri-Mekhmet, in a quenched voice because her small nose was as swollen as her eyes, 'I will do it again. I am very sorry, but I am still unaccustomed to court ways.' She did it again, in a way which made Merenkere lose further height.

'Meri-Mekhmet, my first sister, please get up,' he said desperately.

'How can the King's servant be his first sister, when his own sister is already his Great Royal Wife?' demanded Meri-Mekhmet, staying flat.

'How can *you* speak like that to *me*?' asked Merenkere, kneeling down beside her. 'Meri-Mekhmet?'

'If I have addressed the King wrongly,' said Meri-Mekhmet, rising hurriedly and backing, 'I am truly sorry, O Sovereign, my lord. Please forgive your servant her presumption. Perhaps it should have been your Majesty, or my lord the King? I am a very ignorant girl, as the King understands, since I did not even know him when he visited the house of Ay.' Still she wouldn't look at him. The King stood up too, and stared at her sorrowfully.For someone who had cried a long while she managed to keep her face calmly disdainful, but her full lower lip quivered, as well as her nose tip, which was pink as a rabbit's.

'Meri-Mekhmet,' said the King pleadingly, and tried to take her hand. All his wisdom and dignity deserted him, and he was awkward as the country bumpkin she had thought him. 'I never wanted to make you unhappy. You trusted me. If only your aunt hadn't brought you to my court tonight!'

'Why?' she asked tonelessly. 'So you might continue your double lie? A double land, and a double crown, and – ' She didn't finish, but it was plain she meant 'a double heart'.

'So I might continue to know a little happiness, like other men.'

For the first time Meri-Mekhmet looked at him. She saw he was deeply unhappy, but so was she. He was no longer wearing his head-dress, false beard and lion's tail, but otherwise was still dressed as she had seen him in the throne room. She recalled the first time they had met, and how ignorant she had thought him because he stood there bolt upright and silent; and all the while he had been expecting her obeisance. Then he had amused himself with her simplicity. Her cold hand lay in his like a stone.

'Has your servant her Sovereign's permission to go?' she whispered.

The King stepped back, and loosed her hand. 'Yes,' he said dully. In their first battle she had defeated him, if not finally at least for the time being. He clapped his hands for Hemi. 'Take Meri-Mekhmet to the priestess Tut of Hathor.' As she backed from the room he looked away.

In an outer court the venerable Tut opened her mouth to make some searing comments, but closed it again when she saw Meri-Mekhmet's face, and kept silent. Yet once they reached Ay's house she said, 'You father will still be sleeping, child, so I must insist on knowing what became of you.'

Meri-Mekhmet, like someone talking in her sleep, told her everything. She hadn't bargained for her aunt's delight.

'Of course it was not fair, you silly child! Do you expect kings to be fair? I confess to being worried by this person you called Merenkere. The King's favour is the most important thing that you could have. We are well rid of your country bumpkin.' She gave a rich, satisfied laugh.

'If you speak like that again, I'll kill myself!' cried Meri-Mekhmet. 'You are heartless as the King.' And at the thought of Merenkere's heartlessness she burst into tears once more, and hurried to her room.

The next morning a Palace guard found Meri-Mekhmet's silver bracelet twisted into pieces by the foot of the tamarisk and gave it to Hemi, who took it to the King, who sat and looked at it a long, long time.

Tut, Cat and Jeweller

Meri-Mekhmet lay on her bed and neither spoke nor ate. At midday the Court Chamberlain Ay woke to a household at sixes and sevens. When the priestess of Hathor revealed what had taken place he was very, very angry, and not even the second draught she hurriedly gave him, of crushed scorpions' legs and powdered oryx bone, could calm him. He walked up and down his room cursing her interfering ways and, it must be told, the King.

'Calm yourself, my good brother,' said the priestess Tut, much shocked. 'You will put yourself in danger. Besides, it is all for the best. Was the girl to remain in ignorance always? Now, if we can just get the little fool to see things less tragically, the whole family may profit by it.'

Ay shook his fist in the air. 'I shall resign! I shall go home to my province – '

'This is madness – Sekhmet, goddess of storm and terror, have pity on you! Do you want the King's enmity for life?'

Ay sat down, held his head, and grumbled that he wished only for obscurity.

'Which is the last thing you'll get,' said Tut tartly, 'unless you contrive to disfigure your daughter. Kings' affections do not last, we all know, but while they do it's flying in Hathor's face to resent them.'

'Merenkere's affections may,' said Ay, with a groan.

'You're as bad as your daughter. Idiots, both. You might just as well have been born a field slave. My advice is to exercise your reason, not your feelings, and prevail on Meri-Mekhmet to do likewise. Now, brother, I'm returning to my duties, but if you need my guidance any time you may call on me. I shall leave some powdered serpent's tooth here, which you may use in emergency. Give this amulet to Meri-Mekhmet, with my blessing.'

The priestess Tut, dramatic as only a priestess in a fret can be, swept from her brother's presence, and called her litter bearers. But instead of going direct to the Temple of Hathor she rode to the Palace of White Walls, and asked an immediate audience of the King.

To the surprise of his officials, Merenkere granted her a private one. While the courtesies were taking place he eyed her thoughtfully, decided she knew everything and had come to take advantage of it, and, once they were alone together, came straight to the point by demanding bluntly: 'How is Meri-Mekhmet?'

'O Sovereign, my lord,' Tut lowered her eyes discreetly, 'The child is a little indisposed. The weather is not quite seasonable, and then she was over-excited by her first visit to your Majesty's court.'

'I am sorry. So you came to tell me this?'

The famous directness of touch is really very difficult, thought Tut. Aloud she said: 'O Sovereign, my lord, I would not offend your Majesty. May I have my lord's permission to speak openly?'

The King sighed. 'Do you know, venerable sister, that at least twenty times a day people ask if they may speak openly, and then seize the chance to entertain my Majesty with some grotesque lie? So – since I am devoted to all your house – I do not give permission. I say only, speak as you would to Hathor: that is, the truth.'

Isis protect me from dealing with great men, thought Tut indignantly, I would sooner have a scoundrel any day, one knows where one is with them. She said: 'My lord the King's sister priestess is desolated her Sovereign could ascribe such cunning to her. But your Majesty's servant will be bold. Your Majesty is yet young, so I came to offer my guidance to your Majesty on the matter of dealing with my niece.'

'This is most interesting.' Merenkere's lips twitched slightly. 'I would remind you, priestess, that I have a son and Great Royal Wife, and ninety-three foreign princesses decorate my Majesty's household, as Meri-Mekhmet is fond of pointing out. It is fascinating to know, of course, what advice a dedicated priestess offers on the handling of women.

It is not forgotten, though, that you have Hathor's ear. Speak.'

The priestess Tut, under this gentle baiting, began to wish she hadn't come.

'May your servant presume to ask – O Sovereign, my lord – if the King intends to visit Meri-Mekhmet today, as has been his custom?'

The King narrowed his eyes. 'Why?'

'Because, O Sovereign, my lord, in that case I would beg your Majesty to think twice. Meri-Mekhmet is a foolish, wilful child. She is no doubt longing, as she lies on her bed, to have the chance to play every female trick. She will be ill, she will – forgive your servant – reproach your Majesty, she will undoubtedly beg for crocodiles to end her misery. Ignore her totally, and within the space of a moon she will be waiting in the water garden.'

The King shut his eyes, briefly. He was not an unkind man, but for a space enjoyed a picture of the priestess Tut being chewed by six small crocodiles, and wished himself one of his ancestors who would not have hesitated to arrange it. When he reopened his eyes, he said: 'That would be extremely cruel.'

'Nevertheless, O Sovereign, my lord, it would be common sense.'

'My sister Tut,' said the King silkily, 'my Majesty does not doubt your understanding of your sex, but you do fail to understand Meri-Mekhmet. She would more likely be waiting in Re's barque, than in a water garden. It is my Majesty's opinion that you should keep your energies in future for the Temple rather than waste them in the Palace. The audience is ended.'

Tut prostrated herself. She could have done nothing else, for her knees, like Meri-Mekhmet's the night before, had given way. As she was backing from the Presence the King stayed her with a gesture.

'What news of the Court Chamberlain Ay?'

'He is recovering, your Majesty.'

'Is he calling down curses on his Sovereign's head?'

'O Sovereign, my lord!' gasped the horrified Tut, 'Your servant has never known him do anything but call down blessings on the Sovereign!'

'I would be interested to hear those blessings,' said the King, lapsing from dignity with a sudden grin. 'Didn't I say you would lie to me? Do not be horrified, priestess. I am fond of Ay, he is an honest man, and has good reason to be angry. He might even have courage enough to curse me to my face.'

When she had left, the King sat in heavy thought. He wasn't thinking of her advice, but in spite of longing to see Meri-Mekhmet he guessed it would be useless to visit her that day. So her ordered his servant Hemi to prepare a present of wine and quail for the Court Chamberlain Ay; and then he sent for Reuben.

'You've brought your pipes, Reuben, but do not play just now. Rumour tells me that the sacred cat your friend Tahlevi poached from the Temple of Sekhmet has given birth to kittens. Will you give me the most handsome? Considering it is half mine already,' he added thoughtfully.

Reuben flushed. 'All my animals are yours, O Sovereign, my lord.'

'Pretty words, my friend. I would like to see your face if I asked for Benoni! I want only one kitten. Have them brought, and we will choose the best.'

Meluseth and the three kittens which had travelled to Kemi (two had been left with Shem) were lying in a tangled ball of silk on Thamar's knee. When Hemi appeared Meluseth promptly rolled herself on top of them, so that only one small paw could be seen sticking out from underneath.

'I am not possessive,' she said, 'but I do not like anyone to touch them. Besides, they may catch something in the corridors – I do not mean mice.' When Hemi tried to turn her over she laid back her ears, wrapped her legs round his arm, and dug in claws and teeth.

'Meluseth!' said Thamar. 'You must obey the King.'

'I shall speak to my friend, the goddess Sekhmet,' whimpered Meluseth, holding on like a burr and defying all Hemi's efforts to detach her. 'The King is only a young man, and nothing like so important as a sacred cat; nor does he understand how bad a mother's nerves can be. I shall faint, if anyone touches my kittens.' And she fainted on Hemi's hand, while still digging in her teeth and claws. Thamar herself had to carry the whole bundle of cat and kittens into the royal presence.

'O Sovereign, my lord,' she said nervously, 'I am unable to prostrate myself, or these animals will flatten.'

'The thought shall be taken for the deed,' said the King, who was as amused by Thamar as by Reuben, and found her very attractive. 'Come over here, and let me see them. Sit down on this couch.'

Thamar sat, and Meluseth extended herself on top of the kittens again, and began to purr.

'No good doing that,' said Merenkere severely to her.

Meluseth opened her blue eyes very wide, flirted her whiskers, and regarded the royal hand as she regarded Hemi's arm before she bit it. King's eye and cat's eye met in a tussle of wills; but, before anything disastrous could happen, Reuben leant over Thamar's shoulder from behind, seized Meluseth by the scruff, and whisked her up in the air. The three kittens were revealed looking nervously at royalty.

'Tell me about them,' said the King to Thamar.

'Well, this long-haired white he-cat, my Sovereign, is the only one with Cefalu's green eyes, as you can see. He is good-natured, but as stupid as Mel – as a waterfowl. The black and white female with short hair and blue eyes is intelligent, high-spirited, and will rule anywhere she lives with a stubborn paw. Even Meluseth cannot control her. But the long-haired black he-cat, with Meluseth's eyes and one white whisker, is an almost perfect cat. He is calm, good, noble, well-intentioned, quietly brilliant, affectionate, and at all times in control of every situation.'

'I am overawed,' said the King, 'he should be on the throne. Let me take him.' He picked up the kitten, holding it beneath its front legs, and it swung contentedly from his hands and regarded him with a piercing though honest expression, as if reserving judgement but prepared to think kindly of him.

'Yes, he is full of appeal. I am sure he would well protect any royal house from snakes.' The King swung him to and fro, but the kitten's benevolent expression never changed, although its stomach rumbled. 'Nevertheless, I own to a qualm. Would he supplant me in somebody's affections?'

'Never, O Sovereign, my lord. I forgot to mention that he's gifted with true tact.'

'Thamar!' Reuben's voice was agonized. Merenkere roared with laughter.

'Reuben's wife, I fear you do not think me competition for this creature. It's good to see you show no sign of being corrupted into flattery by my court! Will you put the kitten in a basket, and go with your husband to one of my jewellers, and have him take his best jewelled bracelet, one to fit a young girl's wrist, and place it as a collar round the kitten's neck?'

Thamar went to ask Hemi for a basket, and the King looked at Reuben. 'What is the matter, my musician?'

'Nothing, my lord the King. What could be?'

'I should very much like to know. You do not look as though you approve of me.'

'How should I dare disapprove of my Sovereign, my lord?'

'I'm quite sure you would dare. Come, Reuben, as friend to friend, not subject to King, explain yourself.'

'I do not like to see your Majesty behave as other men,' said Reuben sombrely.

The King raised his eyebrows. 'How am I doing that?'

'By sending jewellery to this young girl, Meri-Mekhmet, O Sovereign, my lord.'

'You have been listening to court gossip.'

'My wife has been listening to court gossip, my lord the King, and one cannot help hearing one's wife, as your Majesty is doubtless aware.'

'I am sending Meri-Mekhmet a cat in a collar,' said the King, exasperated. 'And, my dear friend Reuben, what else am I to do? I'm only trying to make her feel less hurt.'

'She will feel more hurt, not less. At least, that's how my wife Thamar would feel. She would throw it back at me.'

'I am hoping Meri-Mekhmet will have too kind a heart to throw back a defenceless kitten. So perhaps my present will get gathered in as well.'

'If I were my Sovereign, my lord, I would not risk it. I would go myself instead.'

'I shall – tomorrow. Today I send her a cat. You're impossible, Reuben.'

'Only because your Majesty desired me to be so.'

'I did not – I told you to explain your impossibility, which is another matter. But you may find yourself more in sympathy with my new jeweller – a delightful and unusual man. Show him that ring I gave you.' The King gave Reuben his sudden, exceptional smile. 'And when this collar has been fitted, bring it here to me. Now take all these cats away before my lord Vizier arrives. Something possesses him when he sees a cat, and he starts to sneeze.'

Reuben bundled the kittens together, but Meluseth had disappeared. At last they found her in a corner, admiring herself in a sheet of highly polished copper. She had forgotten her offspring, and never noticed one was missing.

'I had not guessed,' she told Reuben as he picked her up, 'that I give off a radiance of pure gold. No wonder they built a Temple to me. Even the King doesn't do that, although he is the son of Re.'

Thamar and Reuben, carrying the kitten, found their way through back streets beyond the Palace to the workshops of the King's new jeweller. An old man scanned them narrowly as they entered, but at sight of the royal ring he bowed himself and led them up a passage to a long, low room, where six men were working with gems and gold and a small furnace for enamelling. They crossed this room, and passed between hangings at one end into a smaller room, empty except for two low couches against opposite walls. Here they waited, while the old man went to fetch his master. In the pause Thamar looked about her.

'It's a humble sort of place, for a King's jeweller.'

'The King likes to tease his court, which is fond of

being grand. This must be the man we've come to see . . .'

They could hear him, because he had a heavy tread. Thump, thump. When he entered they saw why he thumped so much – he was immensely fat, and wore a muffling robe which made him look fatter still. A huge black beard hid most of his lower face, and on his forehead was a sort of copper shield almost hiding his eyes.

'Perhaps he leans over that furnace a lot,' whispered Thamar to Reuben; she was quite unnerved by this sinister presence which seemed so featureless.

'That shield would get very hot,' returned Reuben, wondering why the King had described this vision as delightful.

'Yes? What?' barked the jeweller.

Reuben held out the ring again. 'I am the King's court musician, and have come on my Sovereign's command to – '

'Reuben!' cried Tahlevi joyfully, pushing up his shield.

Concerning a Collar

Tahlevi had sent for beer. When it arrived, foaming in tall clay pots, and they were seated comfortably on the couches, he started to talk; although not before asking after Reuben's and Thamar's fortunes, and hearing something of the tremendous Flood.

'Well, my friends,' he said, as his beer disappeared into his beard, 'this is a remarkable day. And the King is a remarkable man, which I needn't tell you. I expect, though, that you're wondering how I set up in such a respectable trade as . . .' He gestured with his clay pot towards the next room where the six diligent men were at work.

'Indeed, Tahlevi,' grinned Reuben, 'although I strongly hoped to find you again, I am much surprised at the manner of it.'

'One thing follows another, as that noble tomb-robber, my old father, used to say. You remember, Reuben, where you last left me?'

'By the pyramids. Near what you hoped was a concealed north entrance – '

'It was well concealed indeed.' Tahlevi sighed, longingly. 'And yet, you know, my friend, not so

63

well concealed that this acquaintance of yours was unable to spy a certain arrangement of stones and a small crack – in fact, was just running his fingers thoughtfully over it, as you might run yours up and down a flute, when there was an unwelcome cough behind his ear. There stood a most unpleasant priest.' Tahlevi ruminated for a little, nodding his head backwards and forwards so that his beard was tipped with froth from the beer pot.

'You know, my friend,' he continued, 'there are these turning points in life when something happens. A priest's cough may be regarded as a small thing, but it did convince your old acquaintance that nothing could be more unrewarding than brutal death from impalement, such as I had already just escaped.'

'And how did you escape this time?'

'Reuben, to be a successful robber – in fact to be successful – you must know other people. Now, all priests in the Two Lands have a respect for government. Therefore, running my fingers more openly down this crack, and going tck-tck-tck between my teeth, I complained bitterly how the Treasury was always cheated by rascally workmen. I told how the great Vizier Senusmet was grinding his teeth in Mennofer over this very matter. I described myself modestly as sent on a tour of inspection, and I begged that priest to make offerings for my success, so the Vizier might not be further enraged, nor the pyramids breached. I so worked on this poor priest that, almost in tears, he went with me to each pyramid in turn, and between us we not only discovered some secrets still unknown to him, but also found each royal tomb shockingly open to attack. How sadly we parted from each other, lamenting the wickedness of people who could cheat the Lords of Diadems by such bad work! I now knew all I needed – but one thing had happened.'

'What was that, my friend?'

'A priest had coughed. You mightn't think a small cough in the early morning desert could turn a robber into an honest man, but so it was. Some people would say "religious conversion", but I myself think it just bad luck.' Tahlevi sighed, and drained his pot.

'May I have some more of this excellent beer served to you? It comes from the brewery close by.'

They accepted, and when Tahlevi had sent the order, he continued his tale: 'My friends, I was faced with a crisis in my life, and retired into the desert with my brethren to think it over. There it came to me that, knowing as I did so many people who had jewels, or were about to have jewels, or had an excellent notion where jewels could be obtained, I was well fitted – with my natural artistic sense and cunning fingers – to be a jeweller. Also, one of my uncles was already one, in a small way. He was very clever, and could execute any design. A knowledge of jewels, you might say, ran – in one fashion or another – in my family.' He stroked his beard.

'You have a magnificent beard,' said Thamar, who up till now had said little. 'I miss the one Reuben grew on the Ark, since he removed it.'

'Thank you for liking it. At times I'm not very friendly with it – then I remember that priest's cough, and my affection grows. It sprouted fast as lettuce seed in the desert, and when I returned here and found my little shop no one recognized me.' He touched the copper shield above his forehead. 'This I wear whenever strangers are announced, since one cannot be too careful.'

'Tahlevi,' said Reuben, direct, 'can you be sure of your workmen?'

'My dear friend, they are not my relatives for nothing! The impalement of one is the impalement of all.'

'You said no one recognized you? I'm sure the King knows who you are. You should have seen his smile when he sent me here.'

'Yes. To succeed in anything one must be bold, and the first step I took was to make the most beautiful jewelled scarab ring in my power to design, and offer it to his Majesty. Naturally, I didn't expect to enter the god's presence! But he was curious to see a new artist of whom he hadn't heard, and so – ' Tahlevi smiled in his beard. 'No – I did not fool King Meren-kere.' He looked at Reuben. 'All you told me of the King was true. A young man – like ourselves – but already great. He asked me what had caused me to change my craft. I described openly what a priest's cough had done for me. How he laughed! He wished me success in my new life, and was gracious enough not only to accept my ring but have me paid for it. After that, I was made. Once you work for the King

you have not too little work, but too much.' He
smiled again. ' "Doing in the matter of the King's
jewels to the satisfaction of his lord." That is how it
goes.'

The kitten stirred in its basket, and mewed, feeling
bereft of Meluseth. Thamar rubbed it behind the ears,
and it made a small new purr as unsteady as its walk.

'My next customer –' Tahlevi's gigantic frame quivered all over with amusement – 'was my old enemy,
the Vizier Senusmet! To be on the safe side I pleaded
illness, and sent someone else for his commands. He
wanted a necklet of silver, set with stones. I was able
to oblige him with magnificent amethysts. I am told
he wept, for they reminded him of those his dear
mother often wore.' He looked at Reuben with an
innocent stare. 'They were from her tomb.'

'My dear Tahlevi! Your audacity appals me – that
priest should cough again. And you mean to tell me
the *King* countenances this?'

Tahlevi gave a dramatic shudder. Even his beard
looked ashamed. 'Reuben, the King was very angry,
although he may have been secretly amused – it's
common knowledge that he does not love his Vizier;
but his anger, even so, was terrible. He is shrewd as
you said, and guessed what I had done. He remembered I had robbed that tomb – and sent for me.'

'It must have been an interesting audience.'

'Have you seen our Sovereign lose his temper,
Reuben? No?' Tahlevi shuddered again. 'Not many
people have. For myself, I would sooner be impaled
a dozen times over than go through that again. I felt

as though the skin had been flayed off me by his royal tongue. I was lying on the floor at his feet, and he ended calmly: "By right, your King should hand you over to his Vizier, who is also the Chief Justice. What have you to say?" '

'Oh, what had you?' Thamar clutched the kitten to her.

'I was beaten. For the first time here was a man I could admire – not counting yourself, Reuben – and he had convinced me of my crime's enormity; at least, towards him. I said: "My lord the King, your servant deserves to die, if only for abusing your Majesty's patronage. I am at peace if you send me to the Vizier." Although I admit peace was not quite the sensation. "All your goods come from the same sources?" asked the King. "Your Sovereign was regrettably a fool not to have seen you could have come by them no other way." This is part of his greatness, Reuben: he is treated as a god, yet thinks of himself as a man like other men.'

'I know,' said Reuben. 'What then?'

'I had to admit they did. King Merenkere was silent. Then he asked: "And the jewels in this scarab?" "O Sovereign, my lord." I replied, "they came from the High Priest of Sekhmet's brother's tomb – he had the finest taste in jewels of any man your servant can remember." For the first time he smiled. "That man's taste was acquired at the Treasury's expense," he said. "If he had confined himself only to onyx and jasper – ! In this case the King need not worry overmuch. Now, what is to be done with

you?'' He brooded, while your old acquaintance grew
aware of the hardness of the floor and the size of his
own stomach. Then at last the King revealed what
was in his mind. "You are an artist," he said. "Perhaps you could become a great artist. Your Sovereign
cannot employ a dishonest one. Until you're well
established you shall be supported by the Treasury.
But what is to become of these ill-gotten gains of
yours? Obviously, they cannot be returned." Again
he brooded. "You shall make them up," he said at
last, "into the most beautiful things you can design,
and you will sell them; but only to those foreigners
visiting this court whom my officials send you. And
every gold or copper ring of gain you make from
these dealings shall go to feed the poor. Every ring.
Is the matter plain?"

'I could hardly speak. In fact,' said Tahlevi complacently, 'my beard was soaked with tears, it was
quite uncomfortable. I stammered my gratitude,
adding that his Majesty had made me feel I should
really be returning the goods to their rightful owners.
He gave a wry smile, and said that since they came
from the tombs of great nobles or their wives they
were mostly stolen from the Two Lands in the first
place. And he ended with these words, almost man
to man: "Now, do you think, my court jeweller, I
have augmented the priest's cough as a second more
thorough turning-point in your life?" I replied truly
and with emotion, "O Sovereign, my lord, your servant truly believes that if he saw a bracelet lying in
the street he would be unable to bend and pick it

up." "Good," said the King, "you have convinced yourself, at least. Now convince me. If you ever steal again I will myself pick the royal crocodile to swallow you. For your first honest piece of work you may design a necklet for my son, and do not let me find an amethyst in it." With that he ended the audience – which is my story's end as well.'

'Say, rather, its beginning. And Thamar and I have brought you a new chapter. Thamar – let Tahlevi see the kitten.'

Thamar rose and dumped the kitten on Tahlevi's stomach, where it settled comfortably and gave a purr like saws rasping on copper.

'What is this? A kitten requiring jewellery?'

'The King's kitten.' Reuben explained the matter.

Tahlevi looked at him strangely, and then smiled. 'My poor Sovereign, he has failings like other men!'

'To love this girl may be no failing,' said Reuben, 'from what one hears of her. Although he has a Great Royal Wife.'

'I know of Meri-Mekhmet through her father's steward. He calls her tender-hearted and a beauty, but she's also proud. I have just such a bracelet as his Majesty requires; yet I'm loath to put it on this kitten, for fear our Sovereign receives both it and the kitten in his face.' He heaved himself up, and handed the kitten back to Thamar. 'Wait. But if I were him I would send the kitten by itself.'

He went into the other room, and returned with something which he dropped in Thamar's lap. 'There.'

She cried out with pleasure. The bracelet was a beautiful piece of craftmanship: precious silver, set in exquisite taste with turquoise, carnelian and lapis. Yet at once Reuben knew it wouldn't do, though when he tried to find a reason for this feeling he could not. 'Tahlevi, you've always told me you're an artist with your fingers, and it's true in every way. This is wonderful.'

'You really think so, my dear friend? My uncle made it, to my design. You see the clasp can cunningly be fixed so the triple strands become a necklet.'

'It makes me envious.' Thamar shook her head. 'I don't usually want jewels – or not too much. But this – ' She fingered it.

'I would sooner see it on you than on that kitten! If it weren't the King's commission . . . Wait, though.' Tahlevi vanished again into the other room, and returned with a bracelet of as fine work as the other, but in gold, dusted with small pieces of rock crystal, garnets, and agate. 'If you like this, it is my present to you. It's not each day one is reunited with an old friend, and makes – I hope – a new one.'

Thamar could hardly thank him, she was so delighted. Then the King's kitten was fitted with its collar, and Reuben and Thamar returned to the Palace of White Walls with their task accomplished.

Meri-Mekhmet was still lying sadly on her bed, refusing to eat or speak, when the King's messenger reached her father's house. Ay gave the quail and wine a very straight glance, although noting at the same time that the first were plump, and the second perhaps the King's best vintage: sealed with the words 'Vineyard of the Red House of the King's Estate'.

'And what is this?' he inquired, looking at the little basket which had now achieved a lid.

'Most noble Ay, a present from our lord the King to your daughter Meri-Mekhmet.'

Ay coloured like a flamingo. He wasn't pleased by the messenger's glinting, smirking eye. And instead of the expected delight, the unworldly Court Chamberlain expressed himself acidly by saying: 'My daughter is not receiving presents from the Sovereign. There must be some mistake.'

'No mistake at all, estimable one. Perhaps I put the matter badly. It is just a kitten.' The messenger owed his survival at court to his great sense of when to shut his mouth; there was no need to describe what was round the kitten's neck.

Ay's face softened. 'My daughter is unwell, her woman is with her. I will have you admitted. She will see the kitten for herself.' In this way – rather a cowardly one – he hoped to avoid making a decision.

Meri-Mekhmet was taken unawares. When the messenger was admitted she was surprised into sitting up, and speech.

'What is this, Tiya?' she asked the middle-aged woman who sat beside her, holding a plate of sweets and dates she hoped her former nurseling would decide to eat. 'I said no one but yourself should come in here to bother me.'

'Meri-Mekhmet, my dear one, I do not know.' Tiya rose indignantly, and the dates scattered on the floor. 'Be off! Who let you in here? The cheek of it, coming to disturb my mistress when she is unwell!'

The messenger was unperturbed. 'I humbly beg your mistress's pardon,' he advanced with the basket towards Meri-Mekhmet, 'but the Court Chamberlain gave me his permission. I am the bearer of a present from our gracious Sovereign.'

Meri-Mekhmet's mouth fell open. Then she shut it, and bit her lower lip till the blood came. She was silent. The messenger took advantage of her confusion to place the basket on her feet, and unlatch the lid. The kitten, feeling confined, ill used, and desolate for the warm, soft bodies of its brother and sister and Meluseth, climbed unsteadily out, and sat looking at Meri-Mekhmet with dignified unhappiness.

'Take back the King's present to him,' said Meri-Mekhmet in a voice like a sword, as she realized what was round the kitten's neck. She was too late. Her voice, though roughened by tears, was still musical. It was a voice the kitten instinctively knew went with warmth, love and even milk. He began a stout, determined waddle up the bed in a way so appealing that by the time he reached Meri-Mekhmet's knees she had softened, and when he climbed hopefully on to her lap she was undone. Without

73

meaning to she began to stroke his furry back, and the loud uneven purr began.

'Our Sovereign commanded I should beg you, lady, from the kindness of your heart, to care for this poor kitten, which no longer has a home.'

'Oh, surely one could be found for it?'

'That is what our Sovereign lord the King was hoping, when he sent the kitten here.'

'If I do not keep it, no one will put it in the street? Think what the goddess Bast would feel.'

'In spite of the goddess Bast – may she be regarded with awe! – many kittens die,' offered the messenger, with what he felt, correctly, was cunning.

Meri-Mekhmet sat and gazed at the kitten, which gazed back with all its unfair charm. While she looked her heart melted, and she felt a strange softness towards the young Merenkere too. But when she looked at the collar round its neck, so plainly meant for her, cold fury filled her and she would have liked to throw it in his face. She bit her lip again.

'Please wait outside and send in my father's scribe to me. I will accept the King's gift of a kitten, and you may take a written message from me to my lord the King.'

The messenger felt relief spread right through him like the relief from indigestion. He had feared Meri-Mekhmet was going to insult someone; and to bear an insulting verbal message to a sovereign is not a messenger's chief pleasure. He went to call the scribe.

Kuti came, sat cross-legged on the ground by Meri-Mekhmet's bed, prepared his papyrus and ink and poured a libation from his waterbowl. 'To Imhotep, the most famous of scribes,' he murmured.

Meri-Mekhmet took the jewelled collar from the kitten's neck. What had particularly moved her to such fury was the choice of inlay: turquoise, carnelian, lapis; stones the King had worn on anklets and bracelets in his court regalia. ('Does Merenkere think I'm a collar for his ankle?')

'Write,' she told the scribe, 'Most gracious Sovereign and lord King Merenkere, Life, Prosperity, Health, Lord of the Two Lands, Horus of Gold and Beloved of Two Ladies; to her Sovereign his servant Meri-Mekhmet sends profound obeisance and greeting by the hand of the King's messenger. O Sovereign, my lord, she thanks his Majesty for the noble present of a kitten which, since it has no other home, the King's servant Meri-Mekhmet has not the heart to send away. And she returns to her gracious Sovereign the kitten's collar, as a token of safe delivery in the house of Ay; knowing well that his Majesty would find it a more suitable adornment for one of the ninety-three necks of which his Majesty is well aware.'

A King in Conflict

Meri-Mekhmet named the kitten Ptahsuti. She sat on her bed playing with it, and soon it grew startlingly merry and lost its need of Meluseth. But while it played diligently, peering upwards at doves and butterflies painted on the ceiling and thrusting its paws everywhere they would go, its claws were sheathed – for it was, as Thamar had discovered, by nature noble. Its presence comforted Meri-Mekhmet, although constantly reminding her of Merenkere, and its liveliness even made her smile. Sometimes she wondered what had become of her silver bracelet, and would then remember the jewelled one sent her by the King, and suffer a surprising pang of sorrow at the thought of his unhappiness when he received it back.

'So she has thrown it in my face as you expected, my musician.' Merenkere smiled ruefully at Reuben.

'It's the only time I've known my lord the King lack judgement.'

'It would have been better had I let Tahlevi mend her silver bracelet, and sent it back to her.'

'Your Majesty didn't think of it?'

'My Majesty did. Unfortunately my Majesty had already decided to keep that bracelet. Love makes fools and equals of us all, does it not?' said the King bitterly. 'I shall try to see her – tomorrow.'

'Try, O Sovereign, my lord?'

'Should I command her?' the King's smile was as bitter as his voice. 'I am all-powerful. I command every one of my subject's bodies. Not their affections.'

Reuben had a second disturbing intuition, but didn't like to tell the King. Merenkere noticed his expression.

'Speak, man. What is it?'

'My lord the King, your Majesty's love for Meri-Mekhmet must now be known throughout Mennofer, the city being what it is; and – and Meri-Mekhmet's answer.' Reuben saw the King's hand clench, but continued bravely, 'If – I mean, when – '

'You think the people's image of their ruler suffers when they see him as a man who can control his fate no more than other men. Stop having intuitions, Reuben – they're too often right. Nevertheless – I go. Now play to me.'

Reuben did; but after a while Merenkere said, 'It's sad, music no longer makes me happy, only restless.' And he dismissed Reuben, and summoned his Vizier.

The Court Chamberlain Ay was feeling better and thinking he should return to face the King at court, when Merenkere surprised him by walking in behind a flustered slave.

Ay was confused, and hurriedly prostrated himself. He was unwilling to rise and look his Sovereign in the face.

'Raise yourself, my Court Chamberlain,' said the King with the glimmer of a smile. 'Officially my Majesty is somewhere else. Believe me, I am sorry I have caused you some distress.'

'O my lord the King,' puffed Ay, scrambling up. 'There is none, that is, of course – well, Meri-Mekhmet . . .' His honest face puckered, as he tried to think of words that wouldn't make the matter worse. 'Again my – my humble thanks to your Majesty for the delicious gift of quail and – er – wine.' He was so bothered that he absently pressed his stomach and gave a satisfied belch, which he turned into a cough.

'Meri-Mekhmet, on the other hand, returned my gift.'

'Your Majesty?' Ay was horrified. 'But – but, O Sovereign, my lord, there must be some mistake! Meri-Mekhmet is playing with the kitten at this very moment.'

'Ah yes, the kitten.' Merenkere looked at his innocent Chamberlain, and decided he was the only man in Men-nofer who knew nothing of the bracelet. 'I am glad Meri-Mekhmet was pleased with it. Would she come and see me in the water garden?'

Ay said bluntly, 'Your Majesty has only to command her.'

'I am not commanding her. Ask her if she will come.' The King turned on his heel and went towards the garden, where he waited longing to see Meri-Mekhmet, but at the same time wishing himself somewhere else.

Meri-Mekhmet was lying on her back while Ptahsuti slept beneath her chin. She was thinking that she would have her ceiling repainted to a starry heaven: the Abode of the Blessed. Then she would die and go there. Her soul would rise up as a bird and accompany Re's barque as a star. She was just picturing the grim ferryman Turnface or Look-behind who would ferry her – if she was lucky – to join the Just, when her father entered and said nervously: 'Daughter, get up! The King is here.'

Meri-Mekhmet felt herself go weak and cold, and trembled. She held the kitten close, for warmth.

'But I am ill. I cannot see him.'

'You are not ill, and you must.' Ay flapped like a pelican.

Meri-Mekhmet watched him with mistrustful eyes. 'He will send his guards, to drag me to his presence as they did before?'

'He comes as he always did. Alone.'

'And commands me to see him.'

'He does not. He said, "Ask her if she will come." He is in the water garden, by the arbour.' Ay surprised himself suddenly by thinking: He lowers his dignity, just as Reuben had. In spite of Meri-Mekhmet being his daughter he was overcome by male solidarity.

She looked at him and saw his disapproval, and felt sad for Merenkere.

'You lie there and care not what becomes of me!' exploded Ay.

'You are wrong, my father, I do. But the King won't harm you – he is too kind.' She sat up slowly on her bed, dislodging the kitten. 'I will go and see him. Please do not start behaving like Aunt Tut.'

She dressed quickly, and went out. The King was sitting by the pool, staring blankly at her tame heron. As she approached he looked up, but remained where he was. There was the same slightly sad amusement in his face that she had seen before, at the Palace.

'If you prostrate yourself, child, we shall be almost face to face. So I suppose you'll stay upright?'

Meri-Mekhmet stiffened. 'It is as my Sovereign wishes. If your Majesty wants to make a fool of his servant, your Majesty does.'

'You know perfectly well my Majesty wants no such thing. I always like to see you on my own level – not,' added Merenkere wryly, 'that I am not a fool. Will you kneel down, please, Meri-Mekhmet?'

She knelt.

'Closer.'

She shuffled forward on her knees. It was hard to manage gracefully, but she did it.

'Nearer still. There.' Merenkere put his arm round her, but she stayed rigid, staring at the pool, and hurriedly he took his arm way. 'You will now only act as I command?'

'How else should I act?'

'Forget I am your Sovereign. Be yourself.'

'Could I forget?' She looked him in the face. 'Can you really think it possible – your Majesty?'

Merenkere stared at the placid heron. 'You could, if you weren't angry with me, and wanted to make me suffer. I never thought you were unkind.'

Meri-Mekhmet bit her lip, and also stared at the heron. It's impossible to tell what the heron felt; they do not say. 'I cannot forget, O Sovereign, my lord, how your Majesty deceived me. Then you sent me that – that horrid vulgar bracelet – '

A second fleeting look of amusement crossed the King's face. 'My poor jeweller! Yes – that was a mistake, but it wasn't meant to be insulting, Meri-Mekhmet.'

'Everyone in Men-nofer must know the King sends me presents.'

'The acceptance of a King's kitten will scarcely harm you. They also know the King has been rejected.'

She was silent. She couldn't bear this miserable, guarded conversation, where she had been at ease with him before.

'As for deception, you know very well it wasn't deliberate. You didn't recognize me, and – you were young and happy, and – and I – I wanted to feel young and happy, too, not have you thinking all the time about my royalty. *We* were happy, weren't we?'

81

'O Sovereign, my lord – '

'Merenkere.'

'Merenkere, then. Yes. We were happy. But it's over.'

'No.'

'Yes, my lord the King, it is over.'

'Because you're still so angry with me?'

'No – because of your position.'

'Because, really, of the Great Royal Wife, and ninety-three princesses?'

Meri-Mekhmet winced. 'They are ninety-four good reasons.'

'If my sister never existed, and I asked you to be my Great Royal Wife – what of the ninety-three princesses, most of whom were collected for me, like – '

'Like animals. Trapped animals.'

'You're always so complimentary, Meri-Mekhmet, my first sister! Anyway, as I said before, they're simply a tradition, and couldn't be sent back where they came from; it would humiliate them, and cost several minor wars. I needn't accept more, of course, and perhaps the rest would be happy with my Vizier,' he added, suddenly inspired. For the first time Meri-Mekhmet's tragic expression altered, and her lips twitched.

'But your Majesty *has* a Great Royal Wife, and a son. And I'm sure your Majesty doesn't ask anyone to be your wife, you command them. As for your Majesty's Vizier, from what one hears he is unlikely to make anyone happy but himself.'

Merenkere was exasperated. 'It was only a wish, anyway. Meri-Mekhmet, in one minute I shall forget my dignity – and yours – and push you in the pond! And what will you say to that?'

'I shall pull you in as well.' And suddenly she saw him as just himself, and began to laugh. They both laughed; till Merenkere made the mistake of kissing her, when she immediately froze.

'So you really don't want me to come here any more?' he asked sadly. She did want him to, but saw the hopelessness of it, and shook her head. 'No – please don't.'

'All the same, I shall come – every day. You needn't see me, if you don't want to, when I'm here. That's a promise.'

'Then I must tell you, Merenkere, that I shall want to, but I will not come. There are no more king-fishers, you see. He has flown.' Her look challenged him, but she tried not to soften when she saw the expression on his face.

'Nevertheless, I shall come.' The King got up abruptly, and walked away.

He did come. Every day. And every day Meri-Mekhmet lay on her bed of carved ivory with its carved ox-legs, and clutched Ptahsuti to her, and was silent each time Ay told her the King was waiting in the water garden. Poor Ay came to dread these moments when he shuffled between sycomores and sweet-fruit trees to give these stubborn messages. It was not only that he loved the King and disliked seeing him so lost and so unhappy, but he could never quite forget that Merenkere was the most powerful ruler in the world, and a god; and, knowing as he did from personal experience about the frustrations and violence of love, he felt a force must be building up to overwhelm the man in love and reveal the ruler. However sweet his nature, and balanced his character, Merenkere had been accustomed all his life to instant obedience.

There was the Vizier, too. Once Senusmet saw what was happening he asked for immediate audience.

'O Sovereign, my lord, there is an urgent matter affecting your Majesty's whole kingdom. It concerns an – an aspect of rulership.' Senusmet hesitated, which was unusual. The King looked suddenly intent, his Vizier sly. 'Yes, your Majesty. And – and the appearances of power. Your Majesty commands your subjects, does your Majesty not?'

'So my Majesty believes.'

'Would your Majesty say that the question of whether your Majesty commands the wills of your Majesty's subjects rests on the assumption that your Majesty commands each subject separately?'

'I trust my Majesty would not be so long-winded,' said the King gently. 'Or so pompous.'

The Vizier's face darkened. 'All the same, your Majesty admits the argument?'

'My good Senusmet, I am past the age when my advisers seek to school me. But say what's in your mind, and be brief. My Majesty is bored with too much tact – as well as with too little.'

The Vizier said, smoothly and daringly, 'O Sovereign, my lord, it does the Throne no good when the King cannot command *one* subject.'

'Oh?' The King's tone would have made most people change the topic fast.

'Yes, O my lord the King. And when the subject is a woman – '

'My lord Vizier, I appreciate your courage – not your lack of respect for the Throne.' Merenkere rose. Senusmet prostrated himself, and withdrew backwards faster than was customary.

The King was not only very annoyed but – which was unlike him – very agitated. He walked up and down, up and down, and had he worn his lion's tail he would have lashed it. He knew really, deep inside himself, that his Vizier would never have spoken unless he thought the dangers serious. If his warning were ignored Senusmet's loyalty, always uncertain, could lapse entirely. Then he might try to end the dynasty by a Palace coup; or even employ one of the evil potions that the court physicians understood too well. So, thought the King, what would the next step be? Marriage with the Great Royal Wife, which would clear Senusmet's path to the Throne – or at least as Regent to the delicate heir?

'No, no, no!' he said aloud, thinking of his son and the Two Lands in those ruthless, rapacious hands. He sat down again, on a carved ebony chair, and fell into thought. He should never have got himself into this situation. He saw clearly it must stop. The trouble was, he couldn't do without Meri-Mekhmet, though she meant to do without him. For the first time he felt angry with her. She ought to see the harsh demands of his position, and not make them worse by obstinacy. What she was obstinate about, the Great Royal Wife, he – with equal obstinacy – refused to face.

From now on he deserted Ay's water garden, to drive himself and his officials till they were exhausted. There was no more gentle firmness but a grim severity that surprised even the Vizier. Men began to murmur that the Sun was not only Osiris' soul, and in one aspect the kindly Lady of Life, but a destructive force, and to worry in case the old days returned when the word justice equalled ferocity. Once the Vizier had wished to rule with iron, and the King with clemency. Now it seemed they were agreed. Ay, seeing the King's new harshness and the people's fear, thought sadly of his daughter, and shook his head.

When Meri-Mekhmet heard of bloody punishments on hardened criminals, of forced labour for dishonest merchants and lack of leniency to tax evaders, she trembled, clutched Ptahsuti to her, and wondered what had happened to her kind, gentle Merenkere; although she really knew quite well.

'*You* speak to the King,' said Thamar to Reuben, in their own apartments. She was nursing Meluseth, who was again expecting kittens, feeling frail, and constantly speaking of embalmment. 'After all, he is your friend.'

'The King is behaving oddly to his friends, just now.' Reuben had a worried frown. 'These superstitious priests of his all say he is possessed.'

'He's only possessed by love of that stupid girl. Little pig. I wouldn't have minded if you had two thousand wives. Well – not much; not so long as you loved me best. And if the King's unbalanced from sheer unhappiness she's responsible for all that happens, isn't she?'

'He shouldn't have deceived her in the first place.' Reuben fondled Benoni's silky ears. 'That was the real trouble. But I cannot speak to him. In his present mood he'd pay no attention – or look at me as though I were his Vizier.'

'Then I'll speak to him.' Thamar got up, shaking Meluseth off her lap. 'I'll go to him now, and I'll say, look here, you ought not to – '

'Thamar, you'll do no such thing.' Reuben seized her firmly by the wrist. 'What are you thinking of?' And he read her a husbandly lecture about the power and immunity of the Lords of the Two Lands, which glanced straight off her ears.

'Reuben, the world's in the bad state it is because men go on like this the moment their emotions are upset! Wars because someone's kissed someone else, taxes because too many figs upset their stomachs. Where's the King's mother? I could have a word with her, that might be best.'

'She has – as they say here – gone to the West.

87

But it's also said her Ka inhabits a tree in the Palace gardens, unless she's in a lotus or a serpent. You might have a word with her there,' grinned Reuben. 'The High Priest of Ptah would tell you how to find her. You have to take offerings, I believe, and – '

Thamar was looking at him mistrustfully; but just then the King's servant Hemi came to summon Reuben.

Merenkere stood looking out into the gardens. There was a droop to his shoulders, and when he turned Reuben saw a subtle change about his face. It worried him, reminding him of what the foolish priests said about possession. This is the moment, he thought with a flash of horrified insight, when his greatness could turn sour, and when he's old his subjects could curse his name. He was inclined to agree with Thamar in blaming Meri-Mekhmet. A man who carried the King's burdens could not bear them unhappily and quite alone, unless he were made of stone.

'What is the King's will, O Sovereign, my lord?'

'Play for me, Reuben.'

'Does your Majesty mind Benoni's presence? He would follow me, and – '

'You know I never mind. Dog, come here.'

The King sat down, with Benoni at his feet. Reuben sat cross-legged on a rug and prepared to play, but Merenkere raised a hand.

'Why did you look at me as though you were afraid?'

Reuben was confused. 'Did I, your Majesty?'

'Did you? You did. What are they saying in the Two Lands now, I wonder? Well, I will tell you: that the ruler is someone to beware of, a dangerous god, someone with whom men had better not take risks. A short time ago they chattered of things that weren't their business – I have given them something new to talk of, that is all.'

'Is it, your Majesty?' Reuben felt a slight shiver down his spine at his own daring.

The thin, expressive hands on Benoni's head stiffened, and Benoni drew himself away. He sensed some reaction which he didn't like.

'Explain yourself, my musician.'

Reuben hated to explain himself, but saw he must. 'Does your Majesty wish men to talk of tyranny? Of injustice? Doesn't the King of Kemi by tradition stand for Ma'at, or righteousness?'

There was a long, long silence. At last Reuben made himself look up, into the King's eyes. Merenkere was gazing at him with a cold intimidating stare, as though he were a stranger. At last: 'When my Majesty sends for you to play, musician,' said the King softly, 'perhaps in future you will do just that?'

Reuben played. His fingers slipped on the flute, and his heart was not in music. Presently the King said he was exhausted, and had no time these days, and dismissed his former friend without more speech; and on the evening of that day he sent word to the Court Chamberlain Ay that he was straight away to bring his daughter Meri-Mekhmet to the court.

Merenkere, the Ruler

There had been an audience for a savage prince from the strange land of Punt. He had come dressed in skins and ivory anklets, with black hair in ringlets, and a piece of bone stuck clean through his thick though aquiline nose. He was a huge man, tall and muscular, with eyes wild as a panther's, and as cruel. Hardly anyone at Merenkere's court would visit Punt, and once they saw this prince they didn't want to, either. His war canoe had come floating up the Nile as though well used to float between fertile land and great cities; but in fact it was used to jungle, and twining creepers above sluggish waters, or the fast, dreadful boiling of the rapids. He had an interpreter with him, a man who spoke the tongue of Kemi, no one knew how; and his retinue wore ostrich feather shawls, and had square skulls and split ears, and their spears could cut crocodiles in two.

Meri-Mekhmet came to the audience with her father, and as the savage prince left it she saw him stare straight at her with a frankly covetous expression which made her shudder. She was worried enough by the King's summons without having a

90

savage prince look at her as though he'd found her in a tr. p. She slipped behind her father to be hidden from those wild yellow-brown eyes, and was thankful as the room cleared, even though it meant her own meeting with Merenkere must be near.

The Court Chamberlain Ay was dithering and bothering, but beside him stood Aunt Tut who had sensed, with a priestess's sixth sense, that her family connections were at court, and had dared the King's disapproval by turning up to put, as she murmured to her brother, some spirit into her little fool of a niece before it was too late. She hadn't yet understood that Meri-Mekhmet was full of spirit, but the wrong kind for family advancement.

Another Court Chamberlain, a friend of Ay, came to tell them to wait for the Sovereign in an anteroom. He also stared at Meri-Mekhmet, and made a deep inclination before her, and Aunt Tut had already begun to preen herself and mutter praise to Hathor when he told her sharply that the King wished to know why his sister priestess wasn't about her duties in the Temple?

Meri-Mekhmet watched her routed aunt's departure with mixed feelings of relief and dismay. Tut's autocratic ways frightened her, but were at least family backing. She followed her father to the anteroom and stood staring at the fluted columns moulded like papyrus stems, holding up the roof on blossoms, and the gay hangings of woven rushes, and wondered nervously what the King meant by this coming interview. It was all very well to oppose him in the comforting, familiar water garden, but in his Palace and his regalia she felt he would have an advantage. There he was just Merenkere, and here he was the Sovereign; and a divine Sovereign, too. Her hands shook, and her knees wobbled in a distracting way.

'Daughter, I hope you will behave yourself.' Ay was fiddling with a fly whisk, and his voice was glum. 'The Sovereign is the Sovereign, and it's not for you to disobey him, whatever you may think.'

'I will not disobey him if what he wants is right,' said Meri-Mekhmet docilely, and her knees wobbled more. She was glad no one could see them wobble beneath her linen dress.

'There will be no ifs about it,' said Ay firmly. 'Your aunt is quite right, I've been soft with you, and – ' But at that moment a hanging was drawn aside, and the King's guards bowed him into the room. Ay sank on his stomach puffing like a sea creature on land, and Meri-Mekhmet lowered herself gracefully behind him. She heard the ringing sound of the King's titles ' – Son of Re, Lord of the Two Lands, King of the South and North, living for ever!' and then Merenkere's voice telling her to rise. She was alone with him. She had not even seen her father go, escorted by the guards. She stared downward at her feet.

'You have refused to see me all this time, Meri-Mekhmet?'

She swallowed. 'Yes, your Majesty. But your Majesty said I might, and – '

'Perhaps I didn't think you would refuse.'

She said nothing. and held her hands pressed tight together.

'All the same, I kept my promise, did I not? I never commanded you to come and see me in the water garden.'

She was silent. The King came a step nearer. She looked up at him. He was still wearing his full regalia, and this had a chilling effect on her. Yet when she spoke it was defiantly.

'O Sovereign, my lord, your Majesty has commanded me to come and see your Majesty now.'

'Because you've put me in an intolerable position. My subjects are laughing at me.'

'That is all your Majesty cares for? Then your Majesty has only to forget me,' she said in a small voice.

'Do you think that is so easy?'

Her lips went dry. She couldn't speak. She was scared, for there was something strange about Merenkere today – something foreign to his nature. She couldn't know the King himself was scared by his savage sense of strain. The blood throbbed in his head, and he closed his eyes to clear his sight. When he reopened them, and Meri-Mekhmet's face swam clear into focus, her stubborn and withdrawn expression, which he didn't realize was misery, provoked him to rage and a longing to beat down her resistance. As Ay had uneasily foreseen he reacted as a child to her outright disobedience. Suddenly his own helplessness was something he would not endure.

Nor his Vizier's hints and plottings. Nor his intolerable aloneness.

'You and your father shall have rooms in the Palace, then I will see you every day.'

'But – but my father loves his house, O Sovereign, my lord!' she said desperately. 'He – his gardens mean so much to him, and – '

'He may keep them, then.' Merenkere smiled. 'It's not your father I want to see, as you know. Tonight he shall send you to my women's quarters.'

'The King's will is always obeyed, O Sovereign, my lord. And tonight your servant will kill herself.'

They faced each other stonily. Meri-Mekhmet's hands were clenched into fists. She couldn't guess how he was feeling: as though tight bands were fastened round his head, and something entirely outside his control urged him on to be unkind; she saw only that the Merenkere she knew had gone, and she faced a tyrant. She remembered widespread stories about his recent behaviour. He was no longer the man she loved, but a true monster as she once thought.

The King's face altered suddenly, and he groaned. 'How dare you threaten me with that? Aren't I the Sovereign? I thought you loved me, Meri-Mekhmet, but you love only your own will. My Vizier plots against me because of you – he warned me what would happen if I let the people see you disobey. They shall not see. You will do as I say, in future, or – '

'I will not!' Meri-Mekhmet stared at him furiously,

like a child so frightened that it flies into a rage. 'If you're a Sovereign or a god or a beggar I'll have nothing more to do with you, Merenkere, now you've threatened me. I did love you, but I think something possesses you. Something horrible.'

'Control yourself,' said the King icily. 'You don't understand what you are saying – ' He came close and took her by the arm. Meri-Mekhmet wrenched herself free.

'I do understand – I do! And if you think I don't, then this will make you!' She raised her right hand, and struck the King as hard as she could across the cheek.

Then she stood staring at him, horrified. She was only sixteen and she had struck a god. It was sacrilege. There was a dreadful silence, while Merenkere put his hand up to his face where she had struck him.

She was trembling, but still defiant. 'There, now you know what I think of you! Now your Vizier and your people will see I shall be punished! Throw me to your crocodiles, Merenkere – you cannot hurt me m-more . . .' She meant to say it proudly, but her voice wobbled at the thought of crocodiles, and she began to cry.

Her action had shocked the King back to himself. His eyes were sane again, and there was sadness, not madness, in his face.

'You are a foolish child,' he said heavily, 'if you think I could ever punish you, whatever you did, even if you tried to stick a knife in me. Can't you see that you have simply made me desperate? But you mean what you say, so you had better go, Meri-Mekhmet. Never come near me or the Palace again, either you or your father, for I cannot bear it.'

He turned on his heel, and left the room.

After that, the Court Chamberlain Ay took his daughter home. There was silence between them, except when Ay spoke of the charms and seclusion of provincial life, and Meri-Mekhmet cried more bitterly. 'Please, my father,' she sobbed, 'don't decide to leave in such a hurry. You know what regard the King truly has for you – he'll come to himself, and send for you again.' But Ay said bluntly she had changed the King, and no one could tell his future actions. Yet he agreed to wait, and only reproached his daughter in a roundabout way by sighing that they might expect a visit from Tut in her most dragon form.

This made Meri-Mekhmet feel horrible, and once they reached Ay's house she went to her own apartments, where Ptahsuti wobbled forward to meet her hopefully. The sight of him upset her more, but she picked him up and bore him to her bed, where she lay full of self-hatred trying not to think of Merenkere as he looked when she had struck him.

Then the city of Men-nofer and by degrees, as ripples spread outwards, the wide nomes or provinces of the Two Lands suffered under a reign of harshness not known since the King's grandfather was alive. All the petty bullies and tyrants, who had been forced to control themselves during the time of justice and true dealing, perked up their heads and let their real natures free on the poor who had no one now to succour them, since the King had stopped his ears. The arrogance of the High Priests, great officials and tax gatherers knew no limits, and under the King's sombre, silent gaze ferocious judgements went unquestioned or were upheld. Prisoners in gaol trembled, for no sentence was too appalling to be carried out; and the Vizier, at first staggered by Merenkere's actions, came to his unpleasant self, saw the benefits of a free hand from royal clemency, and took the chance to rid himself by all means of his power – which were many – of his enemies.

Tahlevi discussed life with Reuben, as they sat drinking beer in the small room behind his workshop.

'A good thing for you and me the King's passion for this girl didn't unbalance him while we were still in gaol! Your music would win you no royal pardon now, nor me my life.'

'It's a shocking thing to see him so altered,' Reuben sighed. 'At least, it's not so much he's altered; it's as though he were no longer there, and someone else was.'

'This talk of possession all his priests agree on! They seem in no hurry to rid him of it – I think they profit nicely from the confusion. A wise man offends nobody, these days. I must admit, my friend, that had I foreseen *this* I might have set up as jeweller in some other place. What should prevent envious courtiers taking all my jewels, if they can raise stories of dishonesty against me?'

Tahlevi peered anxiously at Reuben.

'I would give them no chance, if I were you.'

'My present is innocent as a baby's smile – did I not promise the King? But I fear someone may come nosing out my past.'

'If they haven't found you out by now, Tahlevi, they never will.'

Tahlevi sniffed doubtfully. 'Anyway, I have you at court to speak for me.'

Reuben's smile was sad. 'For three days now the King ignores me. And before that he treated me to distant courtesy, since I told him his people were worried by injustice.'

Tahlevi looked his admiration. 'You must be the only man in the Two Lands who has ever told that to a Sovereign and survived! In the King's present state I wouldn't mention it again, if I were you.'

'My mouth is closed! Nor shall I have the chance. Did the King return that bracelet?'

'He did. I had it broken up. I'm not superstitious, but it would bring no one luck. Besides, his Majesty would hate to see it elsewhere – or Benoni's mate might have worn it!' jested Tahlevi.

This time, Reuben's smile was grim. 'Then I could well have seen a gaol! But Benoni's mate is causing trouble, anyway. She keeps falling sideways, for no reason. One of the court physicians insists on treating her with magic amulets, but so far he only makes

her bounce. As for Meluseth, I'm afraid the Two
Lands has a bad effect on animals. She wants an
amulet of crystal, carved with a cat's mask to symbol-
ize her old friend the moon. And she talks endlessly
of Re's barque, and sends Cefalu each day to different embalmers to see who could most lavishly pre-
serve her when she dies. He is sick of it. For myself,
I regret my decision to return.'

'I do not regret it, Reuben,' said Tahlevi sincerely.

'And Thamar, much to my surprise, doesn't regret
it. She swears the King's state will soon pass, and
likens it to the madness of bereavement. And she
enjoys a certain favour. Our Sovereign walks with
her in his gardens, and although he speaks little she
says he finds her calming. Well, she was always good
with wild animals.'

'My dear friend, make that remark to no one but
me!' Tahlevi laughed, and rose. 'Forgive me, I have
work to do. Come and see me again soon.' He went
with Reuben to the street. He was puffing.

'Is something wrong, Tahlevi?'

'Merely this intense heat. Our great Nile nears the
start of inundation.' Tahlevi panted. 'There's always
much sickness, and often death, at such a time. The
best advice one can give in this packed city is to keep
cheerful, and stay close until the river's rising is well
under way and the gods are satisfied. Advise Thamar
from me to keep the Palace gardens, and not go out
into the streets where fever is now rife.' He waved
his friend goodbye.

Reuben went to find Thamar. Merenkere had been strolling with her, but had returned to the Palace. Reuben was glad to find his wife alone, now the Sovereign's presence was oppressive.

'Beloved, why have you brought the cats out here?'

'Because they amuse the King, although he doesn't understand their language as we do. He was telling me how Meluseth is a most unusual cat to find here, with her long white fur. You know the Kemi cats are short-haired, and wiry – more like Cefalu, but handsome. Meluseth's ancestor was brought to Merenkere's grandfather as a costly present from some remote country far north-east.'

'Don't tell her so. Think of the result.'

'Alas, she overheard. She has been reminding Cefalu about his lowly origins. It has upset him, you can see.'

Cefalu's tail did look very much annoyed. His neat black nose and scarred ears had an air of arrogant withdrawal.

'Anyway, Reuben,' Thamar sat on a fountain rim and drew him down beside her, 'your friend Tahlevi stole the right cat. He has an instinct for rarity.'

Reuben glanced round him. The garden seemed empty, yet he felt they weren't alone. He often had the sharp intuitions of the desert-dweller. 'Hush, never speak aloud of poor Tahlevi's past. He fears someone may find him out.'

They sat in silence for some while, hearing the song of reeds, the rustle of fountains, the croak of waterbirds. Then Reuben said, sighing: 'It's here I had my first meeting with the King, when the High Priest of Sekhmet gave me to him as a slave. It's hard to believe that enlightened, kindly young man is the melancholy tyrant we know now! I wish things would get better, but I fear they won't. How does he seem today?'

'As charming as you always said he was. It was hard to remember he's the King. But, Reuben, I did try! Then that look came down upon his face which scares us all, and he went away.'

'Did you say something to upset him?' asked Reuben uneasily.

'No, I didn't. He was looking at this pool, and a small red fish swam up, and the King stared down at it – and went away.'

'He used to meet Meri-Mekhmet in her father's water garden. Thamar – ' he dropped his voice – 'do you feel we're alone in this one?'

'I haven't felt so for some time,' replied Thamar tranquilly. 'But no one could be here, except the King's guests or his household – the entrances are so well guarded. Perhaps his Majesty's mother's Ka is up her tamarisk!'

Reuben paid her no attention. 'There *is* someone watching us.' He stood up, and stared around him like a suspicious oryx. Out from a little grove hidden by shrubby bushes walked the Prince of Punt, followed by two retainers. For a short while he stayed motionless, his gaze fixed on Reuben, as though he would commit each feature to his memory. It was a difficult stare to meet, but Reuben managed it. And then, silent as they came, the intruders went, and there was only a faint movement of the bushes, and a bird catapulting itself into the air, to show which way they passed.

'Although they weren't really intruders,' argued Thamar afterwards, 'whatever it felt like to us. He's the King's guest.'

'That man's eyes – those yellow-brown jungle eyes – ' said Reuben thoughtfully, 'are more inhuman than any I have known. They put the Vizier's and Kenamut's to shame, those being just eyes revealing ugly character – but these: they have no character at all, except the emptiness and overpowering threat of great spaces, and forgotten swamps. If I were King I'd send the fellow packing.'

'I don't suppose our poor Sovereign in his present state has paid attention to this Prince at all. Reuben, the King's moods have made you nervous.'

'Perhaps. I wish he would keep his hand steady on his state affairs. I wish he would take notice of these savage visitors – I feel beset by forebodings of danger, Thamar. Do they stem from this man with panther's eyes? I do not know – all I'm sure of is: the King is threatened.'

Thamar's Solution

The heat increased, as the Nile slowly swelled and spread. And then the King fell ill. It was the great time of year, when prosperity should be assured, and when Kemi was crammed with flocking birds – cranes, cormorants, heron, ibises, flamingos, ducks and geese. From dawn till dusk there was a busy flutter of wings all up the river, as nest-building began. But the Lord of the Two Lands seemed to have been struck down symbolically as the waters rose. It was remembered Osiris was both Lord of the Dead and of the fertilizing Nile; people spoke in whispers of his death and resurrection, and turned for comfort to their myths and legends.

At first Merenkere's priests and physicians were hopeful, although there was sickness in the Palace, and several slaves had died. But what might be natural in a slave could scarcely seem natural in a King, and one so young. As Merenkere moved restlessly on his bed all the wiles and wonders of Kemi's chief physicians were brought into play: the spells and amulets, the incense, incantations and charms to ward off evil spirits, the offerings to Imhotep the great father of medicine and demi-god. Towards evening the King grew quieter. One very rare amulet was thought to have improved him, so it was bound to his right hand in spite of all his feeble efforts to resist.

The court was jubilant, except the Vizier, who had secretly drawn up plans for seizing power and the Great Royal Wife; but next day the King was worse: sweat poured off him and he complained of pains in his head and cramps in all his limbs. The amulet was hurriedly removed, in case it was too strong. Still the King grew worse, and at last lay almost on the verge of stupor, his eyes abnormally large in his haggard face. To his watchers it seemed as though he waited for death, and made no effort to escape. The Chief Physician put the valuable amulet away, in case, during some sudden confusion, the Vizier took it. 'When Osiris calls his son, it is useless to oppose,' he said complacently, and added in self-defence: 'His Majesty himself isn't fighting as a young man should.'

From the start of his illness Merenkere had demanded Thamar's presence. He seemed dependent on her, just as Reuben's animals were when they were sick, and lay quieter when she sat beside him - which annoyed all the great men, who felt a god-king should die uncluttered by a court musician's wife. Even Reuben was admitted to the bedside, and received a wavering, forgiving smile; but the King lapsed into lethargy. Once he grew delirious and, bending over him, Thamar heard him arguing pitifully with Meri-Mekhmet, reproaching her. Towards dusk she slipped from the room, and went to find her husband.

'He is dying.' Tears were in her eyes. 'He will die before dawn, if nothing's done except these silly games with amulets. What use is all that superstition?'

'None – but his priests think it helps him, and some of them have secret wisdom. Yet I've always thought the King himself believes more as we do. We can pray for him, Thamar, but what else can be done?'

'I'll go myself and fetch Meri-Mekhmet to him! It's all the fault of that little fool. Why else won't he fight?'

Reuben looked uneasy. 'That might be unwise. There's a rumour he forbade her to come here again, or see him. How do we know what passed between them?'

'Reuben, whatever happens now can hardly make things worse?' coaxed Thamar.

'No – but we cannot take the responsibility.' Reuben was stubborn. 'And she may upset him. I forbid you to – Thamar! Where are you going?'

'Why, the King will miss me . . .' She lowered her lashes meekly, and with a swirl of draperies hurried from the room; but once out of his sight she hurried to an outer court, where she called imperiously for a litter on the King's behalf. As his slaves carried her towards Ay's house she couldn't help smiling, in spite of sadness and urgency, as she thought of past days in the desert, when she went barefoot and was lucky to drink as much as a little goat's milk, or eat some sour curd.

The Court Chamberlain's steward looked at her suspiciously when she demanded to see Meri-Mekhmet.

'It is impossible. The daughter of the most noble Ay sees nobody.'

'Even a Court Chamberlain's daughter obeys the King's command,' said Thamar severely in a voice which contrasted with her gentle look.

Ay's steward squinted slightly. He didn't know her. 'What sign do you show me, O mistress, that it is the King's command?'

'Have you eyes? Aren't these the Sovereign's litter-bearers? She stamped her foot, hard. 'Take me at once to Meri-Mekhmet!' She narrowed her doe's eyes, and glared at him so royally he felt a shiver down his legs, as though a small crocodile had approached him from behind. Hurriedly, without asking further questions, he led her to Meri-Mekhmet's room, where Tiya barred the doorway looking as dragon as Aunt Tut and with an even more insulting sniff.

Thamar drew herself up as tall as she could – which wasn't very tall – and looked Tiya in the eye. There was a battle of eyes. Neither side even blinked. Then suddenly a voice was heard inside the room, saying: 'Tiya! What is it? Who's there?'

'It is a someone who says she's from the King,' said Tiya, in a voice of treason.

'Oh.' There was a long pause. Then: 'What someone?'

'It is a someone called Thamar,' said Tiya in a disowning sort of way.

'Thamar, the Princess of Canaan,' corrected Thamar. Her voice had the beginnings of laughter in it. 'Wife of the King's musician.'

'And you have come from the King, now?'

'Yes – from the Palace,' called Thamar firmly.

'I thought she didn't come from the King.' Tiya folded her arms, and gloated.

'The King didn't send you?' Meri-Mekhmet's voice sounded doubtful. 'Then why do you want to see me?'

Thamar took a deep breath. 'The King will send for no one, any more. He is dying.'

There was a loud, appalled gasp. Then Meri-Mekhmet's voice, thread-like, almost inaudible: 'Let Thamar the wife of Reuben the musician enter, Tiya.'

'But Meri-Mekhmet, my dear one, I – '

'Let her in, Tiya, did you hear me?' Meri-Mekhmet herself drew aside the hangings, and put her hand on Thamar's arm to make her enter. When Tiya tried to follow she was given a slight push in the stomach to send her out again.

Meri-Mekhmet's face was pale, her eyes large with shock, and she was thin from lack of food. Her hair was unbrushed and hung in tangled masses to her waist. Thamar looked at her with pity, but didn't weaken.

'It's not true?' Meri-Mekhmet searched her face

anxiously. 'Merenkere's not really dying? He did send you, didn't he? We knew he was sick, but – he can't, he couldn't be – dying?' She gave a slight sob.

Thamar hardened her heart further.

'Yes, he is dying.'

'Oh *no* . . .' Meri-Mekhmet hid her face in her hands. 'No, no, no, no, no – '

'Yes – he will die tonight, unless you go to him. All his stupid pompous doctors touch him with amulets and mutter spells, but they've sense enough to know he will not fight.'

Meri-Mekhmet wrung her hands. 'He told me never to come there again – He didn't want to see me.'

'Well, he doesn't want that now. He argues with you, and pleads, and – '

'Then he did send, after all?' Meri-Mekhmet looked at her doubtfully. Thamar, who was very tired, lost her temper.

'He did not! He's too ill. Anyway, he knows you're a selfish little pig, and what use is sending for a pig? You knew he was sick – he has been half mad because of you and now he's sick, and even then you didn't try to see him, just to comfort him. I would be ashamed to be you! What good is it to come and ask kindness from a girl who's made of stone, not flesh and blood at all? Now I'm going back to him before he dies, because he's so lonely, and he wants me there.' Thamar turned to go, but Meri-Mekhmet caught her by the arm again.

'Don't go – please don't! I only thought – '

'You thought it was a trap arranged between me
and the King, which just shows – '

'I didn't – I mean, I don't – ' Meri-Mekhmet started
to cry. 'Please wait, I'll come with you at once. Only
say he isn't dying, I can't bear it – '

'I cannot say it. *They* say – his priests and physicians - that he's dying, and I think he may. But it
might depend on you. No, you cannot come like
that! You look madder than he was. . . . You would
frighten him to – even if he wasn't – Call your
woman. Make her do something to your hair, while
I wait outside.'

When Meri-Mekhmet and Thamar at last reached the
Palace they hurried up a side corridor to the ante-
room where court officials and physicians waited.
The atmosphere was one of fluster, yet Meri-Mekhmet noticed nothing but the drawn hangings that hid
the King from her. As she and Thamar crossed the
ante-room she moved slower and slower like someone sleepwalking. Conversation stopped, everyone
stared at her, but this time Meri-Mekhmet was
unconscious of the peering eyes.

They reached the entrance to Merenkere's room.
She turned to Thamar with a frightened face.

'Shall I go in? Will they let me?'

Thamar held her arm. 'Yes – they're accustomed
to my comings and goings. I will take you in, then
leave you there alone with him.'

Meri-Mekhmet drew a deep breath, and together
they crossed the threshold.

The room was filled with clear, close of day light.

There was a choking, fragrant smell of incense burning near the King's bed. Thamar wondered indignantly what good such stifling fumes could do a dying man. Various people stood about the room, including the Vizier, who had eaten nothing since dawn and was now slyly chewing dates. He came forward and subjected the two women to an arrogant stare.

'His Majesty recognizes no one any more,' he said, in his grating voice which already held a touch of complacent kingship. 'He should be left to those who have some reason here.'

'O most noble Senusmet,' responded Thamar sweetly, 'is not his Majesty still Lord of the Two Lands?'

Even the Vizier was unable to say no, since they were surrounded by powerful officials whose support he must win once the King had died. He ground his teeth as though he would like to chew Thamar with the dates.

'The King, when he still knew those around him, wished to see Meri-Mekhmet, the daughter of Ay. He wished to see her,' said Thamar firmly interpreting the King's delirium, 'alone.' She repeated the last word in a ringing voice, to Meri-Mekhmet's amazement, and looked round her pointedly and back, even more pointedly, at the Vizier. Then, somehow, Meri-Mekhmet did find herself alone with the King, except for the Chief Court Physician who was so busy with his incantations he seemed hardly there at all. Even the Vizier had left, grinding dates and his teeth together.

The King's breathing was horribly loud and harsh. She crept forward to stand beside his bed, and looked nervously down at him. Merenkere lay propped up on a pile of soft skins, and cushions, and stared before him as though already withdrawn to some dark underworld. The ruthless expression that had disfigured him was gone, and instead he looked young and vulnerable, and very sad.

Meri-Mekhmet felt terribly afraid. 'Merenkere?' she whispered, and touched his hand.

There was no response. It's too late, she thought desperately, Thamar came too late. She knelt by the bed, and put both her hands over the King's right one which lay palm upward on the coverings.

'Merenkere,' she said louder, and very urgently. '*Merenkere*. It's me – Meri-Mekhmet.' She pressed heavily on his palm, and gazed into his face, willing him to respond. There was still no move of recognition, although the King's breathing changed, and grew quiet.

Time passed, and she stayed crouched by his bed, holding his hand in hers, now and then talking to him as though he were a child. At first the Court Physician's presence made her shy, but then she forgot him altogether – he and his mumblings over amulets and incense and a little figure of Hapy who was god of the river's rising. Once only she looked up to find him there beside her, staring strangely at the King with a piercing, considering stare. Terror made her shake. The King's hand had lain so long in hers she could barely tell if it was warm or cold, for the warmth might be coming from her hands. She moistened her lips and gazed at Merenkere's face. She knew he was dead. The lids had fallen over his eyes. He had never known she still loved him. Tears rolled down her face.

The Court Physician leant forward and very carefully rolled back one of the King's eyelids. He gave a satisfied grunt. 'His Majesty's condition improves. He sleeps.'

Meri-Mekhmet gave a long-drawn, unsteady sigh. 'Will he recover?'

'May the gods permit it! He is very weak. Evil spirits have much hold, and work against me. Yet this time the spell makes him fight – a little.' With a more complacent grunt he returned to his chanting: '. . . an offering which the King gives . . . The gods of Libya and the gods of the Field of Palms come to you.' Meri-Mekhmet recognized an address to Isis.

Throughout the night she leaned crouched by the bedside, stiff and immovable as a statue in a tomb. Sometimes people came into the room, sat, went out again, or stood motionless by her side, yet her position never altered.

Towards dawn there was a difference: the King's hand no longer lay passive under hers, but held it in a close grip. She spoke his name, and suddenly his eyes opened, he moved his head very slightly and looked straight at her. The room was lit by tapers, she saw them as points of flame reflected in his pupils. He smiled, weakly. 'Meri-Mekhmet! You came.'

'I love you!' Her eyes filled with tears. 'O Meren-kere, you must never, never die – I couldn't bear it.'

The King made a great effort. 'I . . . won't . . . die if . . . you . . . stay with me?'

'For always.'

He looked at her searchingly. 'It's . . . a promise?'

'Oh yes, Merenkere, a true promise. Only get well!'

With a sigh the King turned on his side. His hand raised Meri-Mekhmet's and placed it beneath his cheek. He gave a second, more satisfied sigh, and went to sleep.

The Court Physician wandered over to the bed again. He nodded happily, and Meri-Mekhmet heard him murmur: 'Thanks be to Isis. Should be worth an honour from the Sovereign, though how the noble Vizier will express himself . . .'

Next day the King was so much better that the court was agreeably surprised, Senusmet disagreeably. The High Priest of Ptah and the acting High Priest of Sekhmet came to offer their congratulations, and even Aunt Tut came running like a partridge from the Temple of Hathor, with offerings of corn and pomegranates.

Meri-Mekhmet sat by the King all day, till she could keep awake no longer and went to lie down in an adjoining room, while Thamar took her place. But soon the King turned restless, and asked so often for his first sister that she had to return, and slept against his shoulder, looking pale but enchanting, with her mouth wide open like one of Tut's overripe pomegranates.

When Merenkere grew stronger it became clear that – as his court physicians said – his evil spirits had departed. They had left both his body and his mind. He was just as Meri-Mekhmet had known him first, but neither he nor she mentioned her position at the court, and if she would merely rank as a ninety-fourth princess.

Once, when Meri-Mekhmet had left the room for something, the King expressed his gratitude to Thamar.

'She would not have come, without you. Meri-Mekhmet never gave *my* commands any weight at all!' he said, with a slight grin.

'She just wanted her pot down to the bottom,' said Thamar kindly, quoting the country proverb. The King looked unsure of how he liked being compared with a pot, but by this time he allowed Thamar as much freedom as Reuben, and merely smiled, and said that if his own sister weren't already Great Royal Wife things would have been so different. 'But she was always a sickly, melancholy girl, and shy, and even if it were possible I couldn't make her unhappy by discarding her.'

Thamar agreed, and quickly changed the subject. She dared not make the King ill again, with worry, by telling him that both the Great Royal Wife and his son were sick with the same illness which had almost killed him; beset by the evil spirits, said the court physicians, that had been driven from the Sovereign – doubtless determined to wreak their vengeance on his family.

So she tried to make Merenkere laugh by telling him the Court Chamberlain Ay needed an immediate audience, to bring Ptahsuti, who was pining, to Meri-Mekhmet.

'I would not wish poor Ptahsuti to suffer as I did!' smiled the King. So at midday Ay returned triumphantly to court, and Ptahsuti was reunited with his mistress and then wobbled deliberately up Merenkere's bed, and sat down on his chest, and began to lick himself all over in a self-important way.

'I said he should be on the throne,' said the King, 'and see, here he is.' And he laughed with Meri-Mekhmet at the kitten's pride.

PART TWO

The Prince of Punt

A Night of No Moon

The King's son recovered of the sickness that had laid his parents low, to Merenkere's joy; but the Great Royal Wife, after lying several days in a state of mindless high fever, died: too easily, murmured Ay's enemies, though no one, not even those who hated the King in the last days of his harshness, really believed the slander. Merenkere was sincerely grieved for his sister-wife's death, though he could not help rejoicing he was free to marry Meri-Mekhmet as his Great Royal Wife. She, in her turn, was glad they had been reconciled before circumstances made it easy.

The King was still too sick to leave his bed, and all the great arrangements surrounding deaths of royalty were made by the High Priests, the Vizier, and the Court Chamberlains. It was sad the Great Royal Wife had caused more stir in death than in living. For the first time she was noticeable. The embalmers, sculptors, scribes, jewellers, the makers of lovely objects and furniture, occupied themselves with her body, her tomb, and the preparations for her later burial. From all this surprisingly merry bustle Meren-

kere, Meri-Mekhmet, Reuben, Thamar and their animals were isolated by the King's illness, as though
come to rest in a small quiet pool passed by rushing
waters. Anak, Reuben's camel, who was stabled in
the Palace outbuildings with his mate and the elephants, gave his views upon the subject to all who
listened.

'Human beings,' he said, nodding his long neck
up and down in a critical way, 'are so small, weak
and unnoticeable in life, they have to reassure themselves by making all this fuss about it when they die.
Now a camel is so grand, dignified and awe-inspiring
by its nature that its very absence makes a gap
impossible to fill. The whole natural order is shaken
when a camel dies. I need say no more.' He sucked
his teeth, and continued: 'Now as for Cefalu and his
mindless ball of fluff, as our Master rightly calls that
fool Meluseth, they will need all the embalming they
can get, for anyone to notice they have gone. It is
indeed an uneven world.' His mate looked at him in
nervous admiration, but the elephants, caressing
each other lovingly with their trunks, paid no attention. An elephant knows its value, and does not
mention it.

Poor Meluseth was causing some anxiety. Her coat
kept coming out, and she seemed unwell, and tired
easily. She was impatient with her kittens, slapping
them away from her with an angry paw, and she
talked incessantly about the selfishness of he-cats,
and the weariness of bringing yet more kittens into
a difficult world. Sometimes she spoke of the Great

Royal Wife with tender pity, saying that often a lesser light died before a greater. And she consulted the acting High Priest of Sekhmet, a young man with liberal views, on whether her Ka would need a whole tree, or just a small, sweet-smelling bush. Thamar grew so anxious that she took Meluseth to lie on the King's bed, in the hope that grandeur would rouse the will to live; but Meluseth merely lay and looked at him with such sad eyes that Merenkere almost relapsed, and she had to be removed again.

During these days Cefalu often sat rubbing his ugly black head against Reuben's knee in a thoughtful manner. After their voyage in the Ark and the long journey down to Kemi he was quite out of love with Meluseth, and found her frequent vapours and snob-bish ways a nuisance. All round him in Men-nofer there were lissom she-cats, sleek and gay, with eyes like polished obsidian or finely-placed enamel, and whose dark brown or black legs had the natural grace and instinctive posing of true Africans. In spite of Cefalu's plainness they set their hearts on him, for he was of the Palace, high in the King's favour. But Cefalu wasn't interested. He was a cat's cat, and one foolish beauty was enough. He liked to be in his Master's confidence, to run here and there with an air of knowing all about it; tough fights, long adven-tures, the swagger and excitement of midnight encounters with other males under the full moon; and he liked Thamar to stroke and tickle his black plush stomach when he was tired or sick.

'Simple pleasures,' he told Reuben, as he thrust

his head backwards and sideways and forwards, up and down against his Master's knee. 'Simple pleasures, against the background of luxury that is every cat's natural right, are my preference.'

'You're an intelligent, lonely creature, Cefalu.' Reuben stroked the long furry back, pliable as whipcord.

'Solitary, not lonely,' said Cefalu firmly. 'There is a difference. If Meluseth could tone down a little and forget her birth, we could rub along together. Still,' he added, for he was a decent cat, 'I mustn't criticize, and it's good to see Ptahsuti grow to the full flavour of his father's wisdom – '

'You're as conceited as Meluseth.'

'A knowledge of one's own worth is not conceit,' said Cefalu, in a way which reminded Reuben unfortunately of Anak. 'I only consorted with Meluseth as a favour to you, since she was needed on the Ark.' He began a discreet washing of his paw, in order not to see Reuben's amusement at this barefaced lie. 'You must admit, Master, that I'm useful to you. If King Merenkere would give me his confidence, which he does not, I could tell him things to his advantage.' He gave a slight sniff, like the one Meri-Mekhmet used to give at mention of the Sovereign. He was jealous of Merenkere's affection for Benoni, which Reuben knew.

'Such as?'

'Such as: that creature from Punt is up to something. Why does he sneak about the Palace gardens after dark – the usual time for reputable cats to have it to themselves – and gaze up at the latticed windows as though he searched for something he hopes too hard to find?'

'Is it the King's apartments he watches?' asked Reuben uneasily, remembering his own intuition in the gardens.

'Often it is.'

'Since when have you noticed this, Cefalu?'

Cefalu ruminated. 'I cannot tell the exact day. The Prince was there a long while when Meluseth lay on our Sovereign's bed. I hope he doesn't wish to eat her – after all, she is my mate, and the mother of my kittens.'

'He comes alone?'

'No – with two followers. One's so ugly you may have noticed him. A vast stomach, muscles like tree roots, a face which looks as though rolled on by a hippopotamus, and then blown up again like a pig's bladder.'

'I know the man you mean, and his face would frighten children.' Reuben laughed at Cefalu's description. 'He speaks Kemi's tongue quite fluently, while the Prince manages to grunt a word or two. Punt is so very far away that it's odd he knows this language. Your story makes me uneasy, Cefalu. With your leave, I shall tell the King.'

'By all means repeat my words to young Merenkere, if you feel he will benefit,' said Cefalu graciously. 'Alas, he is pigheaded, as one sees from his obstinate affection for that cream-coloured bundle of wool, Benoni: I fear he may not take a sensible cat seriously, but by the feeling in my back legs – a cross between a quiver and a twitch – when I see the Prince of Punt stand beneath a branch where I stretch out communing with the stars and mysteries of night, that untamed wild man with the yellow eyes bodes no one any good. He smells of treachery.'

Cefalu was right. The King smiled at his warning.

'I have no bad reports of this fellow,' he told Reuben, putting an arm round Meri-Mekhmet as she sat beside him on the bed. 'He keeps his followers in good order, is punctual with his tribute, and warmly welcomed our emissaries when they penetrated deep into the Land of Punt some moons ago. Because of this he makes us a friendly visit. His ancestors were not so friendly to my ancestors.'

'I do not like him,' said Meri-Mekhmet, with a shudder. 'He's like a very wild animal. A – a cheetah, perhaps. Nothing friendly, like Reuben's and Thamar's animals. His soul is inhuman, Merenkere. One can see it in his eyes.'

'He is a simple savage.' The King wound her long black hair round his wrist. 'He has seen nothing like the Palace of White Walls, with its windows lit at night and scented trees around it. So he lingers in the garden, open-mouthed. His own palace is made of leaves and mud. I have offered him something to enrich it – the most beautiful rug woven in this city. It will keep us on good terms. Why do you shiver, Meri-Mekhmet?'

'I cannot tell.' She smiled at him. 'I was looking at

the windows - dark with the night sky. And thinking he may be out there at this moment, seeing them lit with life within. Those hard, wild, yellow eyes fixed and beaming towards us out of the dark this minute! I don't like to think what magic they practice down in Punt.'

'Nothing like the magic you practice here,' the King said, kissing her. 'When we can be married I shall give you presents from the Land of Punt. It's always been the land of true romance, you know – my father used to call it "the incense terraces". You shall have gold and incense, fragrant sandalwood inlaid with ebony, a tame baboon, an ivory chair with its seat covered in leopard skin: all from this fellow's cargo. Tell me – where is Ptahsuti?'

Meri-Mekhmet leant down and peered under the bed. 'He was here, a little while ago. Ptahsuti! Suti-suti-su – ' but no kitten came out at her call, and no paw ambushed her hand. The room was searched without result.

'I expect he followed Thamar and Meluseth.'

'No, Reuben.' Meri-Mekhmet was puzzled. 'He wouldn't follow them. Meluseth's quite savage with him, now she expects more kittens. She hits him till he shakes his head with dizziness.'

A second thorough search of the King's apartments proved fruitless. Meri-Mekhmet grew uneasy, in spite of Merenkere's assurance that the kitten was sleeping somewhere in a hidden spot. She said Ptah-suti had taken to playing adventurously in the corridors, and might get lost. Reuben, feeling himself ridiculous, kept thinking of Cefalu's suspicion that the Prince of Punt might eat up Meluseth. He suggested the whole Palace might be searched, without delay. Hemi was sent to order it – still with no result.

'I'll go myself,' said Meri-Mekhmet.

'Yes – but stay in the Palace,' warned the King. She kissed him, and ran from the room. Guards were still searching the long corridors, pulling chairs aside and thrusting spears behind hangings, but they thought all this fuss about a kitten quite absurd, and Meri-Mekhmet saw their zeal increased as she approached and fell off once she passed. My poor Ptah-suti! she thought, and hurried on towards the outer courts. Here one of the Chamberlains assured her the gardens had been searched without success. She thanked him, but went on down to the widest of the garden entrances, and peered out of the colonnaded hall, brightly lit by torches, into the night. How could they have searched such blackness, so quickly, for one small kitten?

The sky glittered with stars, but there was no moon, and light from the torches was lost in shadows so thick they might have been cut from black material. Some way up the hall three soldiers, just come on duty, were reporting to an officer. She thought them lax to leave the entrance unguarded even briefly, and wondered if it was usual, or if she should tell the King. They had not recognized her, for there was none of the obsequious behaviour she had grown accustomed to the last few days. She leant out into the garden, and called softly into the night:

'Ptahsuti – Suti-suti-suti-su . . .' And out of the bushes, somewhere to her left, came a frightened squeak, cut off short, as of a kitten suddenly in pain.

'Oh! Ptahsuti?'

Squeak. Silence. Squeak.

She looked desperately into the dark, then back over her shoulder at the soldiers. They were out of sight, in the guardroom. The long corridor was deserted. She forgot all about the King's words - the bushes were so close! – and taking a deep, determined breath, plunged into the gardens.

It *was* very dark. There were no more squeaks to guide her, and when she reached the bushes she blundered against heavy foliage. Her eyes were dazzled between starry sky and earthy darkness. It was all one muffling mass, with here and there, between leaves, those glittering points of light which throbbed through the air like spear thrusts but illumined nothing. She felt the foliage with her hands. Branches swayed apart at her touch.

'Ptahsuti – ?'

Her left hand encountered air. There was a patch of emptiness between bushes. A path? It was thicker black than all the rest. She hesitated. The squeak came again, louder, straight ahead. She walked into the dark.

Two steps. Three. Four. A tiny squeak sounded almost at her feet. She leant forward, listening. Then the blackness came in close, muffling itself around her. She could feel it with her hands, and it was real. She screamed. The sound broke off short as cloth pressed down over her mouth. She tried to move her feet, but they were tangled in something which pulled them suddenly from under her . . .

Ptahsuti, released from the Prince of Punt's cruel hands, galloped in mad terror towards the Palace, and up the colonnaded hall, his tail stiff and triangular from pain and fright.

'Why, here's Ptahsuti back again,' said Reuben to the King. 'See, O Sovereign, my lord – all his fur stands up as though he was afraid! Has Meluseth attacked him – No,' he bent to peer closer, 'he's been outside. There is a leaf behind one ear – ' he picked it off, carefully, 'and he has a bloodied paw. Has he taken on a grown cat already? Oh Ptahsuti,' he shook his head, 'that was unwise.' The kitten crept beneath Merenkere's bed, and lay there flattened, panting.

'He does seem scared.' The King leant down and looked at him. 'As you say, he has been fighting. No one in Kemi would harm a cat, men have been lynched for it, and they fear the wrath of Bast or Sekhmet. Did Meri-Mekhmet find him, I wonder? Where *is* Meri-Mekhmet?'

They stared at each other.

'Oh my lord the King,' said Hemi's voice from the doorway, 'the Prince of Punt most urgently requires an audience of your Majesty.'

'What, Hemi?' The King stared. 'Tell him to see the Vizier.'

'My Sovereign's orders are obeyed.'

'And find the Princess Meri-Mekhmet for me at

once.' As Hemi withdrew, the King leant back against his cushions, fretting. 'I wish she wouldn't stay away so long.'

But no one could find Meri-Mekhmet, she had vanished like Ptahsuti earlier; and after some while Senusmet himself asked audience of the King.

'Do not bother me with State affairs just now!' said Merenkere frantically, when he was admitted. 'Find the Princess Meri-Mekhmet for me, or keep your face, my good Vizier, from my Majesty's sight.'

'What your servant must reveal, O my lord the King,' said the Vizier ponderously, 'may have some bearing on the matter.' The look on his face annoyed his Sovereign – it showed some secret satisfaction.

'Then speak, man.'

'Your Majesty already knows the Prince of Punt desired audience? It seems he had formed a habit of strolling in the Palace gardens, with his followers. This night he was alone, for his men were occupied in removing that beautiful rug which your Majesty has been graciously pleased to give him. He heard a woman's voice calling for your Majesty's kitten.'

'The Princess Meri-Mekhmet's voice?'

'The Prince of Punt would not know her voice, your Majesty. That is not all, though. One of his men has since told the Prince that, while they were carrying the rug through the grounds, they heard a scuffle some way off in the bushes, and what sounded like a woman's scream. They dropped the rug, and went to look, but it was dark and they saw nothing. Having heard it is the Princess Meri-

Mekhmet who is missing, the Prince demanded audience.'

The King was whiter than at the height of his illness. He threw back his coverings, and got unsteadily out of bed.

'Your Majesty!' The Vizier started forward, but the King waved him aside.

'Convey my gratitude to the Prince of Punt – say my Majesty will see him now. Turn out the Royal Guard to find the Princess – you, Reuben, go and help them.' The King dragged himself shakily to a chair. 'I said the man was loyal . . .'

No intensive searchings revealed a sign of Meri-Mekhmet. The search spread far beyond the Palace gardens, out into the city of Men-nofer, from the nobles' luxurious houses to meaner quarters where mud huts leaned against each other, and soldiers went with caution; and at last it reached the water-front, where out on a dark rippling surface the Prince of Punt's huge war canoe raised its prow insolently into the night. On board it two of the King's men were entertained kindly with a raw gourdful of wine, which they drank sitting on the rolled-up rug pre-sented to the Prince. Then they were shown over the royal canoe, with its rows of grinning oarsmen; and afterwards reported back to the Palace that nowhere, anywhere, had they caught sight of Meri-Mekhmet.

The King was frantic, his sickness reasserted itself, and with difficulty he was prevailed on to stay in bed. Everyone was puzzled and distressed by Meri-

Mekhmet's swift disappearance. It was rumoured she offended Sekhmet. Even a threat of quick acquaintance with royal crocodiles couldn't make the guards outside the Palace gates admit that any strangers had come and gone, or sought to bribe them.

But a short while earlier, before the alarm had reached the waterfront, a second long black shadow of canoe had crept up to Men-nofer out of the deep night. So swift and fleeting had been its coming, so like a pattern flowing on the water, or an unconsidered cloud drifting across a moon, that not even those who lived upon the Nile paid it attention. For a brief while it had tied up beneath the Prince of Punt's bulky vessel, floating under the hull like the canoe's own reflection in miniature; then it had cast off again, moving out of the canal on to the great Nile's surface as secret and unnoticed as it came. The bright-pointed stars were mirrored sharply in the water, till here and there, downstream, they were suddenly extinguished by the passage of a long, thin, black boat, with long, thin oars which stirred up other stars into a dance of sparks, and hurried the boat onwards with the evil scuttling hurry of a spider's legs.

Our Cat in the Palace

Two days and nights passed. There was no sign of Meri-Mekhmet. The King was seriously ill, and the throne threatened. Court rumour said Senusmet was involved in Meri-Mekhmet's disappearance and she was dead; but Aunt Tut, consulting the oracle of Hathor, revealed her niece was living, though somewhere in the dark. This made Merenkere believe she was entombed, and he became delirious. Benoni, who would weigh him down by lying stretched out across his legs to comfort him, was turned from his room, and took refuge with Cefalu on Thamar's and Reuben's bed. Cat and dog discussed the matter in low tones.

'People are not sensible in these affairs,' said Benoni. 'They don't go about with their noses to the ground sniffing, for instance. Nor do they think of consulting us.'

'And if they did consult us, what would you suggest?'

'Not to trust that Prince of Punt, for one thing. He speaks sadly to the King, through the court interpreter – you notice his fat follower, who spoke the tongue, has gone? – yet all the time I smell a secret gloat run through him like a tide.'

'Yes,' said Cefalu thoughtfully, 'and he was quick to bring news of a woman screaming in the gardens; just what might be done, if he wished to throw the blame elsewhere. And does he still stroll nightly by the Palace? I think not.'

'He's too busy showing that ugly face of his within. It's all so open, and I do not trust it.' Benoni put his muzzle on his paws, and his creamy brow wrinkled. 'How can we find the truth for my poor King? The High Priest of Ptah's oracle says Meri-Mekhmet offended the goddess Sekhmet, and has been swallowed by the underworld.'

'Superstitious nonsense.' Cefalu's tail twitched with scorn, also with sudden jealousy. 'My poor King', indeed! He had an inspiration of how he might help the King, but he wouldn't share it. He poured himself off the bed on to the floor, stretched as though his mind was entirely on the stretch, and began to walk away.

Benoni raised his muzzle. 'Where are you going?'

'Oh, nowhere,' said Cefalu carelessly. 'Just to have a few words with our master.'

'Come back if you think of anything,' said Benoni suspiciously.

But Cefalu went from the room making no reply.

He found Reuben by a fountain, and came directly to the point.

'You, Cefalu?' Reuben stared in astonishment. 'Have you overheard something?'

Cefalu's green eyes became slits of vagueness, fixed on inner horizons.

'Cefalu, you are not confiding in me?'

Cefalu yawned, and gazed into the distance. 'It will involve a little excursion,' he said delicately. 'By night. If I do not return, I beg you will make yourself responsible for Meluseth and the kittens.'

'My dear Cefalu, I am seriously alarmed.'

'To danger I say nothing,' went on Cefalu, 'if it will help find Meri-Mekhmet. I ask only two things: first, that my death, should it occur during service to the Two Lands, will be brought to Merenkere's notice.' He wiped his nose solemnly on his paw. 'Second – '

'Second – ?'

'There are twelve strong cats employed on constant Palace mousing.'

'So I have heard.'

'The bag they catch must be a juicy one. I should like all the mice they've caught since yesterday brought to me here.'

'My poor Cefalu, are you hungry? I know the Palace has been very upset, but not that we were starving our – '

'Hunger has nothing to do with it. I wish to choose a fine, ripe, plump, succulent mouse. And on this succulent mouse, Master, may depend both my death and Meri-Mekhmet's life.' Cefalu sank down on his stomach, and tucked his legs beneath him. Then he looked up at the bemused Reuben inquir-

ingly as though to say: 'See to it.' And Reuben, aston-
ished, did.

Twenty-two mice were brought to Cefalu by the
fountain. He discarded ten of them with scorn; spent
some time weeding out another six, and brooded
over the remaining ones, pushing them about
thoughtfully with his nose. At last he indicated his
choice was made, and the gardener might remove
the rest. He waited till nightfall, tense as a spring.
Then he sent a message to Thamar wishing her well,
picked up the succulent mouse, and strode off into
the dark, the tip of his tail twitching in rhythm with
his stride.

He went over the double wall by a tamarisk, haul-
ing himself up the tree paw over paw, running out
along a branch, and taking two stealthy leaps from
narrow top to narrow top. But by the starlight he
saw a cat running away towards the heart of Men-
nofer, and knew he was observed. No cat was ever
killed, no kitten drowned in Men-nofer. The night
was alive with them, the streets awful with howlings
and spittings. A cat at night was protected by the
goddess Sekhmet – goddess of storm and terror –
and not by the more peace-loving Bast. Cefalu knew
with disapproval and some fear that in this town
Sekhmet brought out the worst. There were gangs
of cats near all the temples, cats who boasted they
would stop at nothing. Down on the waterfront they
were unspeakable, ruled by the very worst cat of the
lot: a huge dark cat called Khnum-Put, with three
legs and a wall eye, who had a hundred spies, one

even in the Palace, and was rumoured to have killed near a thousand foes in single combat. His writ ran through the underworld of Men-nofer, the curl of his whisker was dreaded from Ankh-Tawy to the Nile, and it was said nothing went on in the city that he did not know.

Cefalu was challenged at the very first corner. Three cats came tearing out of the dark with drawn claws. They came in silence, swerving slightly to the attack. Cefalu dropped the mouse between his front paws, and waited. When they were close he growled between his teeth: 'Khnum-Put.'

The attack dwindled sideways. One cat ran into the dark, yowling. The other two were not so easily put off. They didn't attack, but when Cefalu resumed his mouse and trotted forward they trotted too, at his heels, and sneering openly. Every few yards, as more cut-throat cats appeared out of the darkness, Cefalu would lay down his mouse and say: 'Khnum-Put'. Attacks dwindled, but his bodyguard grew. Unless Khnum-Put could somehow be induced to offer his protection, Cefalu knew he never would return. The scars on his ears tingled, reminding him of old fights, and battles long ago. He stiffened his spine and trotted on, ignoring his horde of followers. And he made always for the waterfront, where Men-nofer's chief canal led to the wide river.

Attack, attack . . . 'Khnum-Put.'

Now they were so near Khnum-Put's own base that a small spotted cat dashed ahead to warn him and perhaps gain exemption from mouse-tax. Then

they were on open ground, quite close to the high
prow of the Prince of Punt's canoe, rearing dark
against the stars. And there, sitting on a bollard, a
circle of toadying river-cats around him, sat Khnum-
Put himself, watching the approach. Before him, on
its stomach, the spotted cat was giving its report.

Cefalu slowed his steps. He approached like an
ambassador, in a stately manner, staring Khnum-Put
in the eyes, and in front of him bowed slightly, and
delivered the mouse neatly to his feet.

'Tribute, O Khnum-Put.'

Khnum-Put extended a hesitant paw, and turned
the mouse over. There was a small red mark on its
belly, which Cefalu had failed to see.

'This rat was killed by Ti-Keti, our cat in the Palace.
Here is her mark.'

There was a rustle of claws unsheathed behind
Cefalu. He did not turn to see.

Khnum-Put looked at him sternly. 'Why have you
dared bring me a mouse that was anyway my own?'

Cefalu felt his stomach churn, but answered
bravely: 'I had no other mouse to hand, and needed
a passport to your wisdom.'

There was a snicker of glee behind him, and a
sound of claws sharpened on nearby stones.

'Cats have been found in the river for less,' said
Khnum-Put softly. 'For very much less.'

Cefalu felt the circle behind his back starting to
close on him. He kept his eyes steadily on Khnum-
Put. 'I know. Yet the situation in the Palace is
desperate.'

'I have heard of this situation.' Khnum-Put's one good eye was like a knifepoint. 'And it's for this reason that your body, my dear Cefalu, is not even now drifting past the hull of that canoe.'

'You know me?'

'Ti-Keti has described you often. And you were reported as having left the Palace. You are anxious for news of the beautiful Meri-Mekhmet, is it not so?'

Cefalu gave a small gasp, which he turned into a cough. All the same Khnum-Put heard it, and smiled beneath his whiskers. His knifepoint of an eye had clouded with what looked like sentiment. 'Yes,' he said. 'Meri-Mekhmet. What a lovely girl! How tender-hearted. The King has chosen well, he has the approval of all waterfront cats. Do you know, my friend – ' and at the unexpected word 'friend' the closing circle behind Cefalu widened out again – 'that each day in her father's house Meri-Mekhmet would come to the farthest garden wall bringing me plates of delicacies? She had seen my leg was missing – ' he looked round fiercely as though challenging anyone else to notice it – 'and thought I might not fend for myself. Me!' He gave a fierce chuckle. 'They were no ordinary scraps, either,' he went on, 'but the choicest titbits of her father's table. She even offered, from her soft heart, to keep me with her, but it would have been too tame. Now she has a kitten called Ptahsuti. Let no one harm Ptahsuti, or they answer to me for it on the same night.' His whiskers bristled, and the sentiment removed itself sharply from his eye.

'Now,' he turned to Cefalu again, 'you shall have the truth. But never say who told you – or your life's not worth a fishbone. We have one abiding rule here on the waterfront: no outright dealings with the Palace. I make this great exception because you have dared come to me yourself – and about my lovely Meri-Mekhmet. You have guessed who stole her from the palace?'

'The Prince of Punt?' asked Cefalu. 'Yet I cannot see his method. And his war canoe rests here. The King's men have been on board. Only his fattest follower is missing, so far as I can see.'

'Yes, it was the Prince of Punt. He is very clever, and has nicely fooled everyone. Ti-Keti was in the gardens when he abducted her. He laid his trap well, watching every night from the same spot. Ti-Keti tells me he lured her to him by making her follow Ptahsuti's squeaks, when he caught her in a length of black cloth, and with a net for her feet. His followers had the King's gift of a rug near by. A small hole had been made so that she could breathe, then they wrapped it round her and bore it openly past the guards, while the Prince himself went back into the Palace to cause confusion.'

'It is wicked.' Cefalu's whiskers stuck out fiercely and shook. He looked towards the canoe. 'She is still there? But – '

Khnum-Put held up a paw. 'Let me finish. When the King's men arrived, she was already gone.'

'Dead?'

'Oh no, indeed: for the Prince of Punt intends her

for his wife. By now she's two days down the Nile, and closely guarded. I am afraid, my friend, that Meri-Mekhmet, whether she likes it or not, is destined to be Princess of Punt.'

Cefalu gave a growl. It was the only way he could express his fury. 'But if the canoe's still here – '

'I have said the Prince is no fool, savage though he may be. A short time after Meri-Mekhmet, bound in the rug, was brought on board, another canoe, lighter and swifter, tied up alongside. No one else noticed it come or go, for it was very fast, and the night very dark. Meri-Mekhmet was transferred to it, still wrapped like a mummy in the black cloth, and it cast off again, and flew back along the river. I will wager that if anyone stops this craft to examine it they will let it go, for the poor girl will be so closely bandaged, people will think her a corpse to be embalmed! Really,' said Khnum-Put, absently washing over his face with his paw, 'if I didn't so love and admire Meri-Mekhmet I would welcome the Prince of Punt to my own gang: his methods are extremely cunning. For all we know he may make a good husband, too: he seems, now I think it over, to be very like me. Cool, discreet, set on getting what he wants, if a little – firm, shall we say? Yes, she may not, on the whole, have made a bad exchange.'

Seeing the way his thoughts were running, Cefalu decided on discretion. So he thanked Khnum-Put warmly, made a delicate apology for his error of the mouse, and asked for the favour of an escort. There was a slight, unnerving pause. Then Khnum-Put gave a sigh, said, 'Well – it's true, poor girl, she loves the King. And by the way – it's rumoured the Prince follows her in two days' time.' Then, with a wide gesture of his paw, he motioned four strong cats to see Cefalu safely to the Palace. Yet the knifepoint had returned to his eye, and all the way across the waterfront Cefalu, trotting unhurriedly as possible, could feel it bore into the back of his neck between his shoulders, as though at any moment Khnum-Put would change his mind.

Secret Mission

'On these nights of no moon it's good to have company. A little wine?'

'Thank you, but I've had too much already.'

The Captain of the King's ship peered at Reuben anxiously. 'A weak stomach, perhaps? A great bar to enjoyment.' He reached across and refilled his own glass. He belched. 'Now I would say that a little wine, at all times, is of comfort to a man.'

It was Reuben's turn to look anxious. But the Captain seemed fairly sober. A feat, after so many refillings of his glass.

'Your wine is delicious, Captain, but a bee buzzes in my brain, and my belly feels like a distended wineskin.'

'What of it? A passenger may sleep.' The Captain firmly refilled Reuben's glass and, as an afterthought, put the bottle to his own lips. 'A good wine,' he said, smacking them, 'if a little raw. Let us toast Hathor in honour of it.' He drank again, deeply.

Reuben did not drink.

The Captain peered at him. 'You're a foreigner,' he pronounced, nodding his head. 'That's what you are. A stranger within our gates. Won't drink to our loving goddess. Ud push you in river, if y'weren't King's man.' He raised his empty glass towards the sky. 'See her? Over there.'

'I do not see her,' responded Reuben primly, feeling too much wine in his stomach: it gurgled.

'There she is, spread out like a vast cow.' The Captain seized Reuben's arm. 'My friend, this earth of ours lies between her fore and hind feet. Her belly, studded with stars, is heaven's arch.'

'I didn't know it.'

The Captain puffed in a sarcastic way, and the vintage blast nearly knocked Reuben over the side.

'You don't know much, and that's a fact. Have you ever seen a gryphon?'

Reuben thought back to the Ark, and replied: 'They don't exist.'

'That's where you're wrong.' The Captain stabbed the night with an unsteady finger in the direction of the shore. 'Last voyage, about here. My friend, what a sight! Lioness, with a hawk's head and tail ending in a lotus flower. Pretty. Very pretty, if disturbing.' He hiccupped.

Cefalu, crouched under Reuben's legs, looked up with distrust. The reflection of a star shone in one green eye. 'This man drinks too much. He will run us on a shoal.'

'I like you, King's man.' The Captain's eyes suddenly crossed in an emotional way, and he dug Reuben in the ribs. 'What a King, too! Horus of the Horizon, God of the morning sun!'

'Two shoals,' continued Cefalu acidly. 'And he has no true religion. How can our mission succeed?'

'He is a loyal man; be tolerant, Cefalu,' said Reuben; but he removed himself from the Captain's breath and elbows.

The ship was running beneath a sky as black and star-studded as it was on the night of Meri-Mekhmet's abduction. The wind, as usual in this country, was from the north, and blew them helter-skelter down the river. They would sail as far as Coptos, and then Reuben must cross the Eastern Desert by the Wadi Hammamat, and embark in another ship to sail the Red Sea till the coast of Punt was reached. He was entrusted with a desperate mission: to reach the Prince of Punt's capital before the Prince himself, and recapture Meri-Mekhmet in the heart of enemy country.

There had been an alternative. The King could have sent invading forces to fetch her back, while he held the Prince prisoner. It would have been too great a risk. Punt and Kemi would each have held a hostage: and suppose some rival in Punt wished for the Prince's death as heartily as the Vizier wished for his Sovereign's? The death or marriage of Meri-Mekhmet was then certain. And again – the largest punitive force the King could send would easily be lost or beaten in a country so fierce and so unknown as Punt. Those wild highlands and tropical valleys could swallow up an army or protect a foe in a magical, unnerving manner.

So Reuben's mission had been formed, and no one

but Thamar, Hemi, the King and the Captain of the King's ship knew he had slipped out of Men-nofer before dawn, soon after Cefalu had returned to the Palace with Khnum-Put's news. It would be given out Reuben was sick with the sickness that had slain the Great Royal Wife, and Thamar and Hemi were devotedly nursing him. Benoni had been left behind, but Cefalu accompanied his master. He had turned awkward, and threatened to reveal everything unless he could go too. In vain the King had offered to lock him up – Cefalu had slipped out of a window beyond reach, and put his head back to reason with them. He recalled his great success with Aryeh,* and added that a small fleet black animal could be of great use in jungle or highland as a spy. At the last moment the male elephant was taken too, for transport. His size and strength were enormous, yet he could move through thickest undergrowth with amazing silence when he wished. Before dawn he was taken by Hemi a back way through Men-nofer to the ship, and embarked swinging his trunk thoughtfully from side to side. His name was M'tuska.

'Now, King's man,' the Captain attached himself devotedly to Reuben's side again, like a drunk limpet, 'about this secret mission of yours, whatever it may be, I – '

'We must not talk of it,' said Reuben fiercely.

'Of course not, dear friend. As I was saying, this

* See *The Moon in the Cloud*.

secret – wah!' He leapt in the air, and felt his ankle. Cefalu hurriedly resheathed his claws.

'That sobered him, O master,' he purred softly from under Reuben's legs, where the Captain had failed to notice him. The poor man was shaken. Night. Claws. He looked round him wildly, and down; but Cefalu had crept deep into shadow.

'Did you feel anything? King's man?' He clutched his ankle, which welled blood.

'Not I.'

'Nothing clawed you, suddenly, from behind, when we were speaking?'

'I felt not a thing,' said Reuben truly.

'Sekhmet!' whimpered the Captain. 'The King's sister goddess. The lion-headed one. She of storm and terror and the night. Not safe – ' He staggered up, and held his head. 'O Sekhmet – never, never again will I drink a drop on duty. It is a vow. We will turn in now, my friend.' And he staggered heavily away towards his cabin leaving Reuben to seek his own. The helmsman was a silent figure in the dark.

'Did I not say I would be useful?' asked Cefalu, as he curled himself up to sleep on Reuben's chest.

Next day, as the ship continued on its course with the great sail netting the north wind and driving them onwards, it was discovered that all the skins sealing the Captain's winejars were loose, as though someone had broached them with a careful paw; the wine slopped around the scuppers.

'She is a mighty guardian of the King's name, that

one with the lion's head!' The Captain was awe-
struck. In later years this tale got enlarged in the
telling, and included the rising of Sekhmet from the
Nile, the moon shining on her brow, and her swiping
of the Captain into a lengthy swoon with her great
paw-like hand. This caused much sobriety in the
King's fleet.

Reuben had nothing to do but sit all day in his
cabin, and try to form plans for saving Meri-Mekhmet
– though it was hard to foresee how or in what
circumstances he would come up with her abductors;
if he ever did. And what slender resources he had
with him, against the evil force of Punt! A small
quantity of some rare drug known to Kemi's priests,
with which he might tip his spear: if slightly, it would
send the victim into slumber, if heavily, to death;
and some jewels and rings of gold securely hidden
in a linen pocket strapped behind M'tuska's right
ear, for the corrupting of anyone eager and ready to
be corrupted.

When Reuben thought about it all he never
expected to see Thamar again, any more than he
had during his first great journey alone, at Ham's
bidding, into Kemi; in fact, less. Now, as then, he
put his faith in the Lord God of his fathers. Sometimes this was very comforting, and at others he
worried in case the Lord God had some excellent
plan for him elsewhere. As he stroked Cefalu's thick
short coat while the great cat lay stretched out across
his knees, he tried not to remember horrid stories of
sadistic caprices existing down in Punt, where the

Priest-Princes were ruled by strange spirits. Their sorcerers were oracles and rainmakers, and men spoke of their shameful practices in whispers – they were said to put the Vizier's brutalities to shame. I must simply remember, too, he told himself fiercely, that I and Meri-Mekhmet and Cefalu will be more heavily protected –

'It's no good worrying,' said Cefalu, who knew all Reuben's thoughts. 'What will be, will be. Yet we must be careful, Master. There are not only sailors on board, but the Captain has taken a sick traveller too, who keeps the other cabin, and keeps it so close I find it odd. He must be extremely sick, and in that case why hasn't the Captain put him ashore, to seek physicians?'

'What?' Reuben was outraged. 'This is the King's ship! Did this man come on board at Men-nofer?'

'From what I hear, as I go to and fro on board, rubbing myself against the sailors' legs as though I liked them, he has come all the way from the Delta. Rumour has it he also travels by the Wadi Hamma-mat, and takes to the Red Sea for some distant place.'

'My dear Cefalu,' said Reuben, much troubled in his mind, 'how should I do without you? What business had the Captain to take this man on board?'

'None. But when the fellow bribed him in the Delta, he was drunk. He is very penitent now, and very worried, and dare not mention the matter, which is known all over the ship, anyway.' He curled his outer whiskers with a careful paw. 'Did I not say – '

'Yes, you are of great use,' said Reuben heartily. 'But what am I to do now?' He went up on deck, to think it over – avoiding the place in the bows kept empty for an invisible goddess. Really, remembering the myths of Kemi was quite exhausting. He looked up at the sky for inspiration; it gave nothing back but a bright, unfriendly blankness. They were sailing at that moment between yellow cliffs, which sometimes came in close to the river, and sometimes widened out. Here and there, in the valley, groves of date palms fringed the water, or shaded mud hut villages. People stared at the ship, donkeys browsed, naked children played happily beneath an acacia, or basked like little lizards in the sun. Reuben gazed sombrely at these pastoral scenes, and wished himself and Thamar back in their earlier poverty-stricken days. Still, if he died, the King would look after her –

There was a self-conscious cough behind him, and the Captain stood at his elbow.

'Might I put, King's man,' he said in an embarrassed whisper, 'a question?'

'If I may answer it.'

'Well . . . Have you medical knowledge?'

Reuben laughed. 'None to satisfy your countrymen! They rely on magic, on amulets, on spells – unless they're sawing a skull or cutting off a limb. I have knowledge of sick animals; and my common sense.'

The Captain looked round him cautiously and then, still in an undertone, produced the tale Reuben

149

knew already, and added: 'He lies groaning in his cabin, clutching his stomach, which is swollen and painful. I must put him ashore soon, however ill he is, or I'm a ruined man.'

'You were mad to give him passage,' said Reuben sternly.

'I know it – I know it. I'm finished if the truth leaks out on shore.' The Captain blenched. 'Please see what you can do.'

'Impossible. He mustn't know of my presence here.'

The Captain looked more ashamed than ever. 'He already does,' he said bravely, unable to look Reuben in the eye. 'How, I do not know. He conjures information from the air, like magic.'

'He conjures fools from this ship, to tell him. At least, he cannot know my name.' Reuben thought deeply, then said: 'I will see him. It might be better so, now he realizes my presence. Does he know I am the King's messenger?'

'Oh no, my friend. Someone has told him you're a merchant, who travels to mend your fortune with goods from Punt, that is all.'

'A merchant, on a King's ship! Let us hope his wits are dim. One thing this will have taught him anyway – that I'm bound to carry gold, or goods for barter. Now it will be safer if I see him.' Reuben's look was piercing as he added: 'It will go hard with you, Captain, if a private mission for the Sovereign goes unfulfilled because of this.' He followed the nerve-stricken Captain below.

'Who is this man?' he asked outside the cabin. 'What is his name?'

The Captain shook his head. 'He is someone who wished to travel secretly, in haste.' He avoided Reuben's gaze. 'He gave no name.'

'Surely a criminal.' Reuben frowned. He liked this less and less. He gave the rough door a push, and entered, Cefalu like a black question mark at his heels. The man lay with his face to the ship's side, groaning, stretched out on a pile of uncured, smelly skins. His face burrowed sideways, his arms clutched at his stomach. Round his neck, on a chain, was a curiously designed amulet Reuben thought he had seen before.

At the very moment that Cefalu's whiskers stiffened, and his nose began to twitch with animal knowledge, the sick man turned his head towards the door, and stared full at Reuben.

Recognition was mutual, and instant.

It was an old enemy, the former ally of Sekhmet's High Priest; the man who had disappeared so luckily from Kemi before Reuben had returned with Thamar: Kenamut.

Bad Company

Perhaps they were both equally surprised.

'Well,' said Reuben cautiously, after a pause.

'Well, well,' responded Kenamut, clutching his stomach. 'Well, well, well – '

'The Captain says you are ill.'

'Well – I am ill, as you see.' Kenamut gave an unconvincing heave of his whole body, and groaned miserably; but all the time his suspicious eyes never left Reuben's face, as though he would tear secrets from behind it by force of concentration.

'In Men-nofer they believe you dead.' Reuben went over to the attack.

'My dear young friend, what could have – ' groan – 'given you – ' thresh – 'that idea? No, the climate is far better in P – in other places.'

'Far worse, I should have thought.'

'What is worse for some is better for others, if you take my meaning. I also thought you dead.'

'Not at all.'

'So I see.'

The conversation might have ended there, but the Captain took a hand.

'You know each other already?' In his voice sang a note of relief. 'Good. Excellent. In that case, King's – '

'We don't know each other *well*,' intervened Reuben with a frown, though not before Kenamut's ears had pricked. 'Hardly at all. I will try to help this man, Captain, since you must resume your duties.' He stared so pointedly that the Captain left.

'You know something of medicine?' Kenamut panted. At that moment he genuinely writhed.

'Nothing at all,' answered Reuben cheerfully, 'but I'm well accustomed to dosing my animals. Let me see your stomach.'

Kenamut uncovered, and stared at it thoughtfully.

'There are evil spirits in it, and they fight,' he pronounced dolefully. 'But nothing happens.'

'Happens?'

'That should happen, I mean.' Kenamut closed his eyes.

'I see.' Reuben leant over him, and felt the large-domed belly. It was fairly soft, and gurgled whenever he touched it, in a protesting way.

'Where is the pain? On one side? What happens when I press?'

'Ow. It is everywhere. No, not on one side.' Kenamut screwed up his eyes in pain.

'Have you eaten a great deal just lately?'

'There was a tremendous banquet with the Priests of O – with some priests. Yes. Roast goose, stuffed pintail duck, succulent vegetables, wines of all sorts, figs surrounded by – '

'Too much goose, not enough figs or vegetables,' pronounced Reuben, grinning. 'I will concoct something Thamar – that my wife finds helpful in these matters. She has even dosed me with it, under protest.'

'If you knew some magic spells, it might be better.' Kenamut sounded fearful.

'No, it wouldn't; and I know none. You shall have this physic as soon as the Captain's men can find me what you need.'

Reuben went briskly to the cabin door. He felt Kenamut's eyes consider him as he left.

Thamar's concoction was potent. It contained olive oil, fig juice, pounded dates, dill, and some herbs of bitter flavour and quick effect.

The Captain soon came to Reuben with a satisfied expression. 'All is well. The trouble subsides. He asks for you.'

Reuben almost refused. He felt it better to avoid Kenamut. On the other hand, the man already knew him, and it might be wiser to try and bamboozle him face to face than have him ferret out the matter with his uncanny skill. Kenamut could hardly have felt himself in Merenkere's favour, or he would not have disappeared. 'In whose pay is he now?' Reuben asked himself as he went below.

'My dear young friend!' Kenamut greeted him effusively. 'A most effective draught.' He still lay flat on the skins, and his stomach was almost flatter. 'I say nothing about its flavour – ugh! – but its efficiency! I might fancy some of the good Captain's wine.'

154

'That man would be wiser not to drink,' said Reuben feelingly. 'So you're better?'

'Better indeed. What a universal and ingenious young man you are. I may *well* be able to repay you.' Kenamut looked at him narrowly, with the expression Reuben had learnt to dread on his first journey into Kemi. 'Lighten my curiosity. So you were not killed when the people stupidly panicked outside the Temple of Sekhmet. What became of you?'

'I met with old friends, unexpectedly,' evaded Reuben neatly.

'And then?'

'Ah – and then I went north-east again. And now as you see, I am going south.'

'Why, how simply you put it! I might almost think you were hiding something.' Kenamut showed his teeth. The canines were pointed. Reuben regretted not leaving him unphysicked there to groan. He forced a smile. 'There's little to hide, as you may guess. I am going south, to deal in merchandise along the coast.'

'Ah,' said Kenamut, to the gently rocking deck above their heads, 'of course. And if one is a merchant one wishes to buy, or sell; to lose, or – find. You were once much favoured by the King, and this is a King's ship.' He smiled at the deck, as though it might take his point.

'You put it simply, too.' Reuben inwardly cursed the Captain for taking such a passenger. 'Why did you disappear from Kemi? Some said you found disfavour with a goddess.'

'One cannot be in favour with everyone all the while – as you may remember. Some favours are better than others. Some people pay better than others! The King would pay heavily to get his Meri-Mekhmet back again, they tell me. The Prince of Punt would doubtless pay as heavily to keep her. An interesting situation, with different possibilities of outcome, is it not?'

Reuben stared at the swaying boards beneath his feet. 'As a simple merchant I can form no opinion,' he offered weakly.

'Oh, my dear young friend! A simple merchant who travels treated with all honour on the King's ship! A merchant who was once the King's slave and – dare I say? – his friend. A merchant who takes with him jewels for barter, drugs for warfare, and an elephant for transport! I could guess all about your mission before ever I knew who you were or saw your face.'

Reuben got angrily to his feet. It was useless to deny it. Kenamut's abilities had always been uncanny. 'The Captain's men shall stop your mouth for you! After all, I'm beginning to believe you spy for Punt – and you were with the priests of On? So there they entertain the King's enemies behind his Majesty's back.'

'My dear young friend, do not be unwise.' Kenamut crossed his arms above his head, and an inscrutable smile curved his lips. 'All along the route I am watched for – eagerly. It was known in what ship I left the Delta.' He lowered his gaze to Reuben's clouded face. 'People might interest themselves too much in why I disappear,' he said gently. 'Perhaps the King (however big a reward he might offer!) would never see his Meri-Mekhmet in this life again. I wonder what he would offer, by the way? Governorship of a nome? I believe the man who returns Meri-Mekhmet to him may name his own price.'

Reuben was following his own thoughts. 'So you took refuge in Punt, when you found enemies in Kemi. That's how the savage Prince's servant spoke the tongue.'

Kenamut's face set into a snarl, making Reuben realize acutely his own danger. If Kenamut decided to bargain with the King and betray the Prince, then he was no man to share rewards. Once far upon the way to Punt Reuben could easily be blotted out by his old enemy and his old enemy's treasonously treated friends. From now on each step he took must be so wary that he must look all round for traps before he moved. If only Kenamut had died of his sickness!

A smile glinted up at him. Kenamut saw his thought. 'How inconvenient that I survived.'

'You may be of some use,' returned Reuben care-lessly. 'But remember, I'm the King's friend, as you say; and the King has his friends too in Punt, though I shall not tell you who they are.' It was untrue, and to lie made him uncomfortable, but it was the best he could manage – the only thing that might stay Kenamut's hand. He turned on his heel and left the cabin, trying not to hear Kenamut laugh.

Up on deck he was thankful to cool his hot cheeks in the following wind. The great sail billowed above his head, the lotus on the curved prow was beautiful against the sky, the land slipped by on either side, and sailors went to and fro about their tasks. He was surrounded by people, yet alone. After a while he felt something twine a figure of eight about his legs, and looked down to see Cefalu. He squatted on his heels, ran his hand over the short plushy fur, rubbed the scarred ears.

'Where have you been hiding, Cefalu?'

'I made myself into a small pile of fur amongst those skins.' Cefalu blew through his delicately marked nose. 'Faugh! The man stinks. He's so pleased with himself he failed to notice me. Thus I was able to learn things of great value to us. I have earned them, when I think how his feet smelt.' He rose on his hind legs and touched Reuben's knee with an imperative paw. 'At the moment we may put our trust in him.'

'Trust? Trust Kenamut, Cefalu?'

'Trust each man to his advantage,' replied Cefalu impressively, 'and our odorous friend isn't sure where his advantage lies. He talks to himself, as fool dogs like Benoni whimper all manner of things in their sleep.' His whiskers curled scornfully. 'Not a habit with cats, I need hardly say. He cannot decide where he will thrive better: with the King, or Prince. He has thrown in his lot with Punt, but thinks of unthrowing it again – for the King fulfils his bargains, whereas the Prince has been known to accompany gratitude with a spear. On the other hand, Kenamut still has enemies in Kemi who might take revenge on him, if he openly returned. From his mutterings I couldn't make out who they were – only that he means to guide you himself to Punt, and wait on the event.'

'Either way he can dispense with me.'

'Most willingly he would do so tomorrow. He hates you for the high favour you stand in. A small splash in the river, or more likely a sudden disappearance in the jungle – Yet you needn't fear at present, Master. If he decides to steal Meri-Mekhmet back he will want your help at first – and your elephant. Rest easy: from all I learn, he will not move at present.'

He crouched down at Reuben's feet, and his green eyes blinked.

'I wonder, will I see my bold son Ptahsuti again? Still, a warrior cat must take his chance.'

'Thank you, my good Cefalu. I'm greatly in your debt.' Reuben stroked Cefalu tenderly, and sighed. 'I wonder what Thamar – what they're all doing in the Palace now?

They were worrying. The Prince of Punt had disappeared a day earlier than expected. And Meluseth, whose limpness and ill health still caused anxiety, had taken to seeing visions, which she said foreshadowed her end. One night she saw herself drawing Re's barque through the underworld. She talked in dreams with the King's mother's Ka under the tamarisk tree, and brought back an urgent message that Merenkere was to sip dill water slowly, mixed with powdered scarab – which, when tried, brought him out in spots.

'Now look what you've caused!' said Thamar indignantly; but Meluseth only replied it was better to have spots out than in, doubtless what the former Queen meant.

Her last vision was thoroughly disquieting. It took place just before daybreak. The Palace was roused by her plaintive cries. In a terrible dream she had seen the Prince of Punt surrounded by the evil powers of Set. He was armed, his eyes shot yellow fire. At his feet stood a cat with three legs, whose one good eye was sharp as a knife point. There was some sort of bird crying 'Treachery!' in the distance – perhaps the ibis-headed god of wisdom, Thoth. Horror, Meluseth shakily explained, had brooded over the entire scene. She was convinced she would never see Cefalu again, and Meri-Mekhmet and Reuben were certainly in danger.

'It's quite wrong to upset everyone like this,' said Thamar in double indignation; but she privately sent someone to the waterfront, who returned with a report that the Prince of Punt's great war canoe had gone already.

'But he cannot leave without taking farewell of his overlord, the King!' moaned the Court Chamberlain Ay, flapping his hands up and down with distress. He had aged since his beloved daughter's disappearance, and his skin hung on him loosely, like an old man's.

'It has taken place according to prophecy,' said Meluseth dolefully but with some pride. She was sipping warm milk fortified with wine.

Thamar looked at her disapprovingly. 'Can't you stop prophesying?'

'You forget I had a temple of my own,' replied Meluseth with dignity. 'We who are chosen by gods cannot choose when they make their visitations, whatever lesser people think. The Prince of Punt is gone, and that is that. O wretched day', and she fell into a swoon.

The King, although weak and feverish, had held his ground, sustained by frail hopes of Reuben's mission. But Thamar brooded anxiously over him, and did her best to keep Meluseth's depressing forecasts secret. However, that the Prince had slipped away was a State matter, and couldn't be kept hidden. The Vizier Senusmet suggested a fast vessel should be sent to bring him back, but this might have led to war, and had serious results for Meri-Mekhmet. That night the King was worse, Benoni scathing in his denunciations of cats, Senusmet hopeful of the throne. The Court Chamberlain Ay's flesh hung on him more obviously than ever. If Reuben had been able to see them all it would not have raised his spirits; not one bit.

Luckily, he couldn't. And he was far too busy to think about the Palace now, or even his beloved Thamar: the King's ship had reached Coptos, where they disembarked for the land journey to the Red

Sea. They said goodbye to a shamefaced Captain, and joined a caravan of merchants with their donkeys, which reminded Cefalu of his first journey down to Kemi.

'You know, Master,' he confided to Reuben – they were both poised on M'tuska's head, out of Kenamut's earshot: he preferred donkeyback travel – 'this meeting with our old enemy may be of heaven, after all. It strikes me we're very noticeable with our elephant. Whereas if this fellow Kenamut is expected, as he says, no one will think twice about us in his company. Also, I'm sure he still has uneasy feelings, that I came from his lion goddess. I've noticed certain humble motions of the spine in my presence.'

'Yes – and what he tells me, though alarming, is useful too. For instance, I was puzzled how the Prince's men could transport that canoe with Meri-Mekhmet across the Wadi to the Red Sea. No one had seen it at Coptos, which worried me. However, Kenamut assures me the Prince's ships came straight up a branch of the Nile, which has been thought almost impassible, with all those cataracts! Kenamut describes it as powerful magic, which makes him afraid, but I suspect those men are just brilliant oarsmen, who know their light craft in a way we cannot. My heart's filled with distress for poor Meri-Mekhmet in the terrors she must be undergoing! Her savage, cruel companions, the boiling of the waters, the fear of the unknown! And the fear, too, that no one has found out where she is. I'm afraid it may well drive her mad – and if she tries to escape it will only make matters worse, for we shall never find her and she'll surely die.' He sighed. 'The very best we can hope for is to catch up with her in the Prince's capital, before he can arrive.'

Cefalu pondered. He wondered if he would worry Reuben with his thoughts. In the end he decided not to hide them.

'Do you know, O Master, what god the people of Kemi say dwells at the Nile's first cataract – according to Kenamut?'

'One needn't pay attention to their gods, if one's own heart is right,' said Reuben stoutly.

'Nevertheless, O Master, there is dark coincidence here; and beyond the first cataract, which puts a barrier between the King of Kemi and the violent, mysterious land of Punt, all may be said to work on the savage Prince's side. That evil god is called *Khnum*.' A slight shudder went through Cefalu, as he remembered the knife-sharp glint in Khnum-Put's eyes. Khnum-Put lived by the Nile, a cat born and bred in its mysteries. Cefalu's was no vision, like Meluseth's, but he felt deep within him that the Prince of Punt was not too far behind them in the chase – the high prow of his war canoe heading down the Nile, to shoot the terrible cataracts in all its pagan pride.

M'bu

Meri-Mekhmet's terror was quite as great as anyone could imagine. She was half dead with terror, and her savage companions managed her easily enough for, like an animal in extreme fear, she became limp and motionless and her limbs hardly seemed her own.

Khnum-Put had been right, and till they were well past the first cataract and heading rapidly into the unknown she was mostly kept bound and bandaged almost like a mummy. Her situation was curious: she was both a captive completely in her captors' power and, as the Prince's destined wife, an almost sacred possession. So she was tied up yet treated with deference. This last was something to be thankful for, since the Prince's ugliest retainer, the one aptly described by Cefalu as having a face which might have been rolled on by a hippopotamus, a man of iron strength, was as pleased by her as both the Prince and King Merenkere; and if he hadn't been scared of his own ruler might not have confined himself to feeding her against her will with a horrible concoction of stale meal mixed with water, and a form of palm wine which, once tasted, she never wanted to taste again.

At first she thought that she would die of terror, and not see the King till he too had taken the journey along the dark river of the underworld. She was glad, for though she might be searched for far and near, how could her searchers ever guess what had become of her? If she had only stayed safely in the Palace, as Merenkere told her! Then she realized she was too young and strong to die of fear, and a worse fear settled on her, as N'mumba the hippopotamus-faced described her future, secluded in the Prince's great grass and mud compound, and having many children for the tribe. At first he was surprised by her revulsion, and then amused, and then he took pleasure in teasing her with tales of the Prince's eagerness.

'He coming on trail, two three days now. Ceremony take place soon he come. Much dance, drink in honour – please people much Prince he have heir. You very pretty for Prince, he please much steal King's wife! King he too proud, think Kemi too strong. He not so proud when Prince him steal his wife.' N'mumba gave a wide grin, and paddled her face with huge fingers as though she was an animal. Meri-Mekhmet just restrained herself from biting them off.

'Your Prince will have war with Kemi!' she told him proudly. 'The King will utterly destroy him.'

N'mumba laughed. 'Prince love two things; love women, love fight. Fight for woman, that please him. Your King how he destroy my Prince? He know our mountains, our jungles, sicknesses our gods bring for enemies when we dance, drum, drink in gods' honour? Whole army vanish seeking you, never find, never, never. You not know way we guard prisoners! Princess – you learn.'

Meri-Mekhmet, whose courage had revived when she just stopped herself biting him, felt faint again. How could even Hathor help her now? She thought of worldly Aunt Tut, and wondered if Tut herself believed in Hathor. The great goddess of Kemi seemed suddenly a flimsy creature of imagination. Then, to her surprise, she thought of Reuben – almost as though she could hear his voice, see his face. Reuben had been protected, had survived almost as bad a journey as her own. This led her on to thinking of the God of Reuben's fathers, who had brought Noah and Reuben through a flood, and defeated the High Priests of Sekhmet and Ptah. And the priests of Kemi, skilled in strong magic, were not primitive sorcerers as the Prince's priests must be. All at once she felt a strange sense of comfort that made her strong.

During the following days she needed all her strength. She even drank the hated palm wine eagerly, since food and drink were scarce on this long journey. The Prince's servants drove their canoe as fast as they could. They had been told not to delay where unexpected pursuit might find them. So there was no hunting for meat in the land they passed through, though sometimes there was a piece of speared raw fish, quite disgusting to Meri-Mekhmet

– it was a peasant's food, one she had never eaten. And there was that endless stale, watery meal.

With each stretch of river passed – sometimes slow-gliding and calm, sometimes boiling against half-hidden rocks – it grew more obvious how useless an escape would be. If she ever doubted it the sight of crocodiles basking on mud banks, or coiling watersnakes swimming with their heads above water, changed her mind. As for the land on either side which, after the desert, was sometimes gaunt and mountainous with a mere fringe of vegetation, at others a thick mass of steamy jungle, there hundreds of undreamt-of dangers must be lurking.

Now and then she saw people at the water's edge, or small canoes would feather along level with their own but out of range, like pilot fish leading a great shark. These people were so different from her own that they merely increased her dismay. They watched like shadows of darkness from the bank: creatures of the wilderness, of whose existence she had hardly dreamed – so primitive, her own civilization had passed their stage thousands of years ago, before Kemi emerged from mists of time. Locked behind barriers of their own strange thoughts and tongue they would be far more foreign to her than Reuben's animals. To escape among them would be more terrifying than staying where she was.

'Perhaps the Prince will not escape from Kemi!' she said boldly to N'mumba. He laughed. 'Princess, you not know my Prince. When he not come, then

I, N'mumba, marry you!' and he laughed again to
see her shudder.

'I will kill myself!' she said passionately. That was
a mistake, for he was worried, and re-bound her
wrists with grass ropes, and pinioned her securely
to her seat; then he grew still more interested in her,
and would sit for hours stroking her hair or her face,
and roar with laughter when she tried to pull away.
As they went further from the Prince his deference
was growing less.

After days and days of travel they reached a great
lake reflecting skies of deep, vast, tropical blue. The
river flowed into the lake, and was lost in it; and the
canoe travelled on across the surface, along a path
of hidden, swift-moving current. The canoe's many
rowers made a sound they thought was song, but
to Meri-Mekhmet was like the rhythmic barking of
baboons: a savage grunting and wailing which
seemed to fill the earth and sky.

'We reach Prince's people,' said N'mumba happily;
and Meri-Mekhmet's heart turned cold as stone.
What is homecoming to one is death to another.

On the great lake's opposite side a wide stream
flowed out of it which bore the canoe onwards while
the oarsmen feathered to keep within the current.
So in time they passed between marshes with stark
reedbeds, and saw more mountains savagely guard-
ing the skyline, and ahead of them a lush tropical
valley full of heavy jungly growth and great trees
hung with creepers. There was a vile-smelling creek
winding eastward, overhung by creeper thick as tan-

gled snakes; and in the trees themselves snakes rustled, or hung like creeper. Up this sullen creek N'mumba's men poled their craft, with Meri-Mekhmet shrinking from fleshy leaves trailing across her face. The crude song rang out; and the day was blue twilight amongst stinking, mysterious vegetation, for the worshipped sun of Kemi was quite cast out from this hidden world.

N'mumba grew ever more cheerful, as his broad face looked round lovingly at his home ground. 'Hai!' he said, 'nowhere else like, in world.' Which Meri-Mekhmet hoped was true.

At last the creek widened. They reached a rickety landing-stage made of roughly shaped logs bound together. Other canoes were tied to it, or lay pulled up on shore. Theirs was made fast, and then N'mumba picked up Meri-Mekhmet, flung her over his shoulder, and started off on a path well-known to him – though to any stranger this slight wandering way between trees and undergrowth would have been invisible. His men followed in silence. The only sounds were an occasional weird cry of some jungle bird or a monkey's chatter as it swung from tree to tree, and the pervading, monotonous whine of many insects.

'Terrible country, Kemi,' said N'mumba. 'Fine, here.'

Meri-Mekhmet, who was hanging upside-down anyway, did not reply.

They reached a giant clearing. Round its edge was a stockade built of reeds. Within was a circle of huts with makeshift appearance, as though someone had hurriedly moulded them from mud. Right in the centre was one large, imposing, oblong dwelling, balanced on four poles, with rough steps to a small squat doorway. As N'mumba and his men approached, the clearing filled silently with people. They came from the huts and jungle itself, and drew silently round him and his burden as dogs circle a strange beast. N'mumba paid them no attention. He shouldered his way past, while they fell back as though afraid. He bore Meri-Mekhmet to the steps and up them, and into the dwelling which seemed empty. The floor was covered with dried reeds. In the centre lay a pile of skins. N'mumba deposited Meri-Mekhmet there, and unbound her wrists. At first she could see little till her eyes grew accustomed to the darkness, which was not so great as it might have been, because of holes in the reed-thatched roof.

'This is the Prince's palace?' she asked, rubbing at her wrists. She did not trouble to hide her contempt.

N'mumba gave a huge bellylaugh which made her shrink away. 'This! This one secret ceremony place of all Princes. Safe, no enemy here.' He looked round him gladly, said 'Hai!' on a grunt of satisfaction, and went to the entrance.

'One come, with food,' he said, looking back at her. 'Then, one come.' He went out. Meri-Mekhmet stayed where he had put her. She was without hope. Without memory or thought of Reuben's god. There was nothing left but to kill herself, and now there seemed no way to do it. What spurious comfort that had been, on the river! And there she might have accomplished death – might have thrown herself sideways from the craft, been caught by crocodiles before she could be reached. How could she kill herself here? Perhaps, when night came, she could creep away into the jungle, till she died. But she knew inwardly she was too well guarded to escape. Well, then – she would starve. Yes, when food came, she would not eat.

It was brought by a young girl, whose smooth brown body was naked, her hair a mass of plaited strands tortured over bone pins; one pin was stuck through her nose. Meri-Mekhmet shuddered. She must die before the Prince came, or he might stick one through hers. Although the food smelt possible – it was roast fish with honey and fruit – she waved it away. The girl misunderstood. She placed it on the floor, then bent forward and stroked Meri-Mekhmet's long hair as though it surprised her, and went away.

Meri-Mekhmet tried not to look at the fruit and honey, for she was hungry, but she couldn't help sniffing like a famished dog. She sat there beside temptation a long time. The hut's atmosphere was hot and moist, and smelt of turbulent jungle growth. She knew there were many people outside, but the silence was oppressive. The words 'one come' kept going through her mind. What had N'mumba meant? Not the Prince, already?

The footsteps were so soft they were merely part

of the jungle sound pattern. Suddenly there was someone in the doorway. Meri-Mekhmet gave a small scream, which she silenced with her hand.

A woman stood there, a strong woman of middle age, whose drooping breasts were bare and fell nearly to her waist. Her hair stuck out in a frizzed mass all round her squarish head. The face itself looked as though carved from ebony: wide, dry, wooden lips, a long wooden nose flat between her cheeks, a chin falling away towards a neck circleted with many bone necklets. Unlike the girl who brought food she wore a skirt of dried reeds which made a great bell like a small thatched hut beneath her hips. Round her waist was a thong. From it dangled the wizened bodies of dead snakes; and twisted all up her left arm, its head nodding near her shoulder, was another snake, copper-coloured and very much alive. The woman's eyes were bright with hatred. Till she looked into those eyes Meri-Mekhmet had not guessed that, though the Price desired her for his wife, his people might object. The wise woman M'bu objected very much.

'Hai, daughter from Kemi,' she said in Kemi's speech; and spat. 'Make welcome.' She gave a terrible smile.

Meri-Mekhmet could not speak.

'Prince, he think please people. He people not pleased. Yet he obey. You not eat?'

'I will not eat,' replied Meri-Mekhmet proudly.

Once more, that smile. The woman swayed backwards and forwards in the entrance, backwards and forwards. The snake swayed on her arm, and lifted its head to her ear, and touched it as though kissing. 'You eat.'

'No, I will not.'

'Prince, he angry. Look at me, daughter from Kemi.' Meri-Mekhmet looked. She couldn't take her eyes away from the dreadful sight. M'bu swayed more vigorously. She half closed her eyes and stared into Meri-Mekhmet's. They were slits of darkness, they were dark light, there was no centre to them, just a drawing into darkness. Meri-Mekhmet looked and looked and couldn't look away. It was as though a frozen hand was on the back of her neck, forcing her to look. The eyes were all-commanding. They were out there looking at her – then they were inside her own head, looking out. 'Give me back my eyes!' cried Meri-Mekhmet suddenly, desperately. She knew her own eyes had been taken from her head, and others put there. Eyes that saw things in a different way.

'What eyes?' asked M'bu softly, still swaying. Meri-Mekhmet put her hands up over her eyes which were not hers. How could she even remember what she asked for – ?

'You eat now, Prince's wife,' said M'bu. Meri-Mekhmet hesitantly picked up the roast fish. Somewhere, distantly, she still knew she must not, yet she ate the food that would give her life.

'You eat all.'

There were no scraps left. Not one. M'bu gave a

grunt. 'What you want now, daughter? You want knife?'

'Yes – give it me!' Meri-Mekhmet stretched out a hand; the other still rubbed at the eyes so strangely not her own.

'What you do? What you make with knife, heuh?'

Meri-Mekhmet only knew she wanted it. She stretched out a pleading hand. It was as though M'bu made no movement – yet, suddenly, there was a knife glinting with its point stuck in the floor by Meri-Mekhmet's hand.

'Want knife, daughter?' asked M'bu, evilly amused.

'Eyes, *they* want knife?'

And Meri-Mekhmet's hand was frozen, as the back of her neck had been. She couldn't move it near her body. Her fingers opened, the longed-for knife dropped from her hand. She stared at M'bu, puzzled, and could remember nothing.

'So. I take you from yourself,' said M'bu softly, 'till you called in calling rite, for Prince. You no more here. You in jungle, in dark. You in prison, place of great tree. You eyes alone in dark, look for way back. Never find, till I, M'bu, call! Look up, daughter, with eyes I give you.' Meri-Mekhmet raised her stranger's eyes and looked, as through great distances and deep water, at a giant snake hanging its head down from coils high in the roof. Those snaky eyes were the third eyes of M'bu. They did not even frighten her.

'Sleep,' came M'bu's voice from beyond horizons far away, 'sleep.' The voice was like a tide falling over her. Under its tremendous power Meri-Mekh-met crawled on to the pile of skins, and lay face downwards, and slept. The snake fell to the floor beside her, and coiled its tail around her feet.

The woman M'bu stood and looked at her with hatred, turned on silent ebony feet, and went out.

She said to N'mumba, in their own tongue, 'I have done. She sleeps until I call her. Even if Kemi's magic steals her back again, it will never steal her eyes, herself, from where I hide them. Our Prince is obeyed, yet I do not like it. This woman brings some sorrow to our tribe.'

The Still Small Voice

On the long journey Reuben took his different path with Kenamut. He fretted to hurry, for Cefalu's forebodings about Khnum-Put had transferred themselves to him, and each time he lay down to sleep he shut his eyes on a picture of the Prince's great war canoe thrusting its way down river, flying by night and day towards its goal, earlier than they expected.

He listened impatiently and with one ear to Kenamut talking about Punt's riches, and the strange exotic land itself – its huge range of climate, its marshes, mountains and jungles. Incense and sandalwood, said Kenamut, giraffes, baboons, panther and leopard skins. Ivory, he whispered gloatingly – and gold. But Reuben could think of only one thing Punt should render up – Meri-Mekhmet.

And at last, after many days, they were in Punt. Not just its border, but the interior itself, and going ever deeper towards rescue or capture. Then all three were glad of M'tuska, whose enormous feet swung silently forward across mountain flank or scrubby marsh, desert border or tropical valley; and Reuben was even glad of Kenamut. Whatever the dangers of his presence, without him the venture would have been impossible. They had to admire the way he could adapt himself. He might have lived in Punt all his life, instead of having fled there as a fugitive such a short while before. No doubt the Prince had welcomed him for his usefulness and firsthand knowledge of Kemi, his intimate contacts right up to the Delta – even so, what he knew already was astounding. He guided them unerringly.

'When we reach the Prince's capital – '

'Ah – that we shall not reach,' replied Kenamut.

Cefalu unsheathed his claws and tapped them thoughtfully on M'tuska's neck.

'No – here we have to guess, and must hope our guess is right. The Princes of Punt have a secret ceremony place, not shown to strangers. It is here, my dear young friend, we may find they have taken Meri-Mekhmet. I shall be interested,' Kenamut smirked, 'to watch you rescue her.'

'This man is treacherous,' growled Cefalu. 'He will guide us to a trap. How can he know a place not shown to strangers?'

'How do you know this place, Kenamut?'

Kenamut's lips came upwards into the straight line that was his smile.

'Let us say I have my intuitions. One who has been high in the counsel of Kemi's High Priests has his methods. All great Punt occasions, it's said, take place near this sinister creek where we're going. Naturally, I've not penetrated this sacred spot myself, but I shall regard your progress, my dear young friend, with interest, while I put this question to myself: for whom is Meri-Mekhmet born, the Prince of Punt, or the King of Kemi? You see, these things should not be interfered with, or there's trouble. And I will warn you, to avoid trouble for us both, that we're going to the dark centre of Punt's magic. Don't laugh, my friend – what I have seen done in Kemi is nothing to what I have seen done in Punt. Yes, I, Kenamut, have trembled! These people are very close to the earth. Their gods are demons of the forest, and pagan ancestors with horrible desires. Have you ever, in the pretty gardens of Kemi, heard of the wise woman M'bu?'

'Not I.'

Kenamut looked round him. They were passing through a jungly place, with pools of stagnant water, and thick undergrowth. At the name of 'M'bu' it seemed the creepers swung towards them, like snakes. As though the undergrowth was someone's ears, and listened.

'They say in Punt,' he whispered hoarsely, 'that though the Prince rules, all the power of the land is locked up in this woman and her ancestors. She is its guardian, its force. Without her rites the crops fail, cattle perish, the children die, enemies triumph. She has strong magic. She can take the souls of men from their bodies, and leave them empty husks, walking but dead. I have myself seen her servants. They are silent, with dead eyes. Where does she send the Ka, when she takes it from the body? No one knows, and some of the guesses are too terrible to be repeated. One thing I will tell you, though – and you may discover what it means. Somewhere in the forest is a tree, and a guardian of the tree, who keeps the eyes of M'bu.' Kenamut gave a mocking laugh, then looked round nervously; which was not lost on Reuben. 'That is why, my dear young friend,' he concluded, 'I shall not come with you quite *all* the way, though I shall be glad indeed to hear how you progress. Take care you do not spend your life as M'bu's slave, with dead eyes. As for cats - there's nothing she likes better than roast cat, since she seldom gets one.'

'You've not yet decided which side you're on, have you?'

'It is the most unsubtle thing to take sides, till one is sure which is the right.'

'Which side is winning.'

Kenamut said nothing, but his eyes expressed in turn anger, jealousy, deceit, arrogance, uncertainty, natural treachery and hatred. After which they were so tired they crossed.

'If the woman M'bu takes away your eyes I will ask for you as slave,' was all he said.

'And if she takes yours, I will deal likewise,' returned Reuben.

Open enmity declared, they journeyed in silence. There was now not far to go, which was a good thing, since enmity on an elephant is difficult. They were penetrating a valley downwards, into the deep floor of the jungle. Overhead the creepers twined so thick they made the sky invisible; it might not have existed, nor the distant range of soul-uplifting mountains. Sometimes there was a slithery movement above them, which was a snake; or a monkey chattered in amazement at the elephant's passing.

'Stop now,' said Kenamut.

They stopped. There was total, eerie silence.

'The ears of M'bu listen,' whispered Kenamut. 'Now your way lies straight on, towards the creek. You will stumble on a stockade.'

'What should I do then?' asked Reuben, at a loss.

If Kenamut had dared he would have laughed again, but just then he was too frightened, and deeply regretting the greed that had made him come. 'Sell them your wares – merchant! I do not think you will deceive the wise woman. I await you here – but if I see your eyes anywhere about . . .'

He dropped from M'tuska's back, and was lost in the jungle.

'I admit to a slight sense of worry.' Cefalu stretched out his paws shakily on M'tuska's head, and dug in his claws to steady himself.

'Dear Cefalu! I am glad to share it with you.'

Reuben listened. The silence was utter, profound.

M'tuska stood quite still, swaying his huge bulk from side to side. His trunk examined a creeper, gingerly.

Reuben unhitched a spear from his side, took a small leather bag from his waist, and tipped the spear with dark ointment. It was all the preparation he could make, and not suitable for a merchant, anyway.

'Dear Master, before we move,' said Cefalu, 'may I ask you for one favour? When it seems I may be roast, would you touch me with that spear of yours?'

'If there's a chance, Cefalu, yes. But you forget I may not have my eyes.' Reuben touched the spear's haft to M'tuska's flank.

'Forward.'

In her hut, behind the stockade, the wise woman M'bu crouched statue-still upon the ground. She stared into a gourd held by her left hand. A smile re-carved her wooden lips.

'The Prince comes,' she murmured aloud. 'He nears the great lake.'

Her slaves paid no attention. They were unaware of anything but her commands. They swept the ground beside her, they prepared her food. They did all with wide, staring eyes which held nothing but emptiness. There was a Syrian merchant amongst them, whose light skin looked strange in this dark hut. He had come to barter, and been too inquisitive. It amused M'bu. She had her light prankish moments, and decided he should be her dog. He barked when spoken to, slept across her feet at night, gnawed bones she threw him, and scratched himself with his feet.

A slave spilt something near her, and prostrated himself for forgiveness. M'bu ignored him. She still stared into the gourd, but her smile had gone. She raised her head, and swivelled it until her face was turned east, swinging it as though searching the air. She gave a deep, ferocious grunt. Her eyes closed.

'What comes? What comes?'

Then her eyes opened. They fixed. A darkness rose behind them, out of the spirit of the ages, and they began to draw, and draw, and draw . . .

'Something horrible is happening,' said Cefalu suddenly.

It was true. All round them the fleshy leaves and creepers were pointing one way, as though pulled by a current.

'Do you feel it?' He clung to the elephant's head. His tail was pulled forward over his spine. The elephant's ears billowed as if a wind blew behind them. A monkey went past as though someone had thrown it.

'O God of my fathers!' cried Reuben aloud. He had prayed often, all through this journey. Never so desperately as now. 'O God of my fathers, beyond that stockade is something terrible! So terrible, it's drawing strength from my bones. Yet we must go there. Protect us. Save Meri-Mekhmet . . .'

All round them the drawing continued. Yet now M'tuska's ears were limp against his head, and Cefalu's tail fell back to its normal position.

'O Lord of Lords . . .' prayed the shaken Reuben, as the drawing howled in the leaves, but no longer touched the travellers. M'tuska rocked to a standstill.

'We must still go forward, friends,' urged Reuben stoutly.

Then something happened to him. It was an experience he himself had never had before, although it quite often happened to old man Noah. A great inner stillness fell on his spirit. It was as though circles of light began spreading outwards inside him . . .

'Master!' said Cefalu, awed.

'Hush,' murmured Reuben.

The light spread. There were inner ripples, indescribable, a cross between colour and sound, followed by a still small voice, speaking with quiet authority.

'Not that way, Reuben. That way surely leads to death. Turn north, my servant. North, to the great tree. And be of strong courage. Once the guardian of that great tree is destroyed, there shall be no more fear.'

'North, O Lord?' stammered Reuben, 'but – '

'North, my servant. And quickly.' The voice took on a peremptory note. Reuben bowed himself over the elephant's neck, and the inner light faded, and went. Cefalu was staring up at him in astonishment. Without waiting for commands M'tuska turned, and plunged into the jungle on their right, where the leaves hung still.

Outside her hut the wise woman M'bu stood shaking her head from side to side, puzzled. There had been something, and now was nothing; only a few monkeys and snakes blown into the stockade by a high wind – good for eating, but little else. She turned her head sideways, left, right, swinging it to and fro as a pointer swings his nose to pick up a scent. Nothing. She cast wide. Still the same. Never before had the dark spirits behind her been mistaken.

She went to the great hut, climbed the steps, looked in.

Meri-Mekhmet lay asleep, the snake coiled around her legs. It raised its head to watch M'bu with calm, obedient eyes that were the Syrian merchant's.

All was well here. She climbed down again. She looked into her gourd, and saw the Prince of Punt's canoe come ever closer, gliding across the great lake.

'All is well,' she said to the hippopotamus-faced N'mumba, 'he will be here before dark. And yet, and yet – ' and she raised her carved face, puzzled, to the sky.

Tree of Eyes

The elephant seemed to know his way unerringly. He went with no guidance from Reuben, who sat erect and allowed himself to be carried with Cefalu towards the north. The jungle was thicker here, the land sloping downwards, the silence more profound. There was a darkness beneath leaves that was unnatural, and it moved under creepers like water flowing. They rode for some way, while the air grew heavier and heavier, and eventually turned to mist around them. It too was unnatural, not rising from damp or water: a mist of darkness which sought to choke the intruders. Reuben began to cough, and Cefalu to retch.

'Are you sure we're going – ' he began, when Reuben countered: 'Stop!' and held up a hand for silence.

He had heard something: a weird, intermittent sound as though someone was letting jets of steam escape from pans of boiling water, and then stopping it with a finger. A 'hsss-s, hsss-s, hsss-s' which grew louder and louder as they advanced. Cefalu began to shiver up his spine and his tail expanded like a bottle brush. M'tuska quivered over all his bulk, but bravely advanced. Reuben wished he felt himself as courageous as the still small voice expected of him. He would have given much to be elsewhere.

All at once there was the inner light, and the voice spoke gently but firmly. 'The trial has come,' it said, 'be strong and of a brave heart', and went again, and at that moment the elephant floundered on to the verge of a clearing, and came to a halt, swinging his trunk from side to side.

There was no mist here. The ground was hard and bare. There was little light, for high up – a long way up – creepers and branches from all round the clearing met together in the centre, at one great tall tree. Its trunk was oddly lumpy, Reuben thought. He raised his eyes, and had a shock. All the branches and creepers were alive with snakes. They coiled or writhed, or lay there watching him. Their eyes were human eyes.

Cefalu gave a small mew of dismay – cats do catch snakes, but not so many – and Reuben's hand gently soothed his spine, but his gaze was drawn back to the tree trunk. It was grey: a thick, dingy grey; and broken all the way up by thicker lumpy bands of black – diagonal, diagonally moving. With a head –

It was the biggest, most powerful snake Reuben had ever seen. A giant among snakes, a snaky snake that expressed all snakes. It was moving round and round the tree, and now its head came into view again, and began to pull out away from the tree's trunk towards them, with a 'hsss-s, hsss-s' that was the sound they had heard.

'Help!' cried Cefalu, losing his nerve for the first time in his life. M'tuska was cast in a mould of fear. Reuben himself was fascinated into stillness by the horrible triangular head, the coiling black body, the flickering tongue that now darted in and out, in and out, on air midway between him and the tree –

In one sudden movement he leapt to the ground, raised his poisoned spear, and stood alert.

The hissing stopped. The head made some sudden feinting, darting movements, then withdrew a little, while the black body further unwound itself, preparing for attack.

Reuben balanced the spear. Drew back his arm, and –

And before he could throw, the black coils moved faster, poured themselves across the gap, and wound themselves round him as they had round the tree, diagonally, until the hideous head waved level with his eyes – and his spear arm was bound to his side, with the spear knocked pointing downwards.

Reuben felt the most terrible fear and loathing he had ever known in his whole life. The head waved to and fro triumphantly in front of him, the coils tightened. All the other snakes began pouring from the branches and creepers, came slithering down the tree trunk to help their lord finish his prey . . .

With a despairing effort Reuben flexed the muscles of his right arm, and managed to dig the spear's tip into a fat black coil.

For a moment, nothing happened. Then the triumphant 'hsss-s, hsss-s', stopped. The snake's mouth opened, as though trying to rid itself of something. Reuben could see right down the throat. There was a sudden slithery loosening of the coils about his body, and then the reptile slumped to the ground in a tremendous heap. Its muscles, convulsed by the death agony, caused it to thresh the earth with its whole length, so that a loud drumming sound echoed through the jungle, and faded away. Except for a few violent quivers, it was still.

Reuben stared at the snake's head, and raised his spear to strike again, for certainty. Its eyes looked back into his. They were Meri-Mekhmet's eyes, crying with fathomless sorrow. He stared at them, horrified, wondering what he had done. Then he saw it must have been some strange illusion: the eyes were green eyes, snake's eyes, glazed in death.

All round the clearing dead and dying snakes dropped to the ground in a soft, snaky rain, with squishy thudding sounds. Their human eyes were gone. They too were only snakes.

Reuben stood there, dazed and weak-kneed. He could scarcely believe what had happened. He stared round him – stared at the tree. The thick, dingy grey bark appeared to crumble, the creepers drooped, a fierce ray of sun pierced the gloom and lit the top, which began to burn and shoot out flames.

'The great monster is dead,' cried Reuben aloud, as though he must prove it to himself. He plucked his spear from the snaky coils, and walked back to

Smoke writhed round it and up, just as the tree's guardian had wound itself around the tree, till suddenly a high wind rose and blew it away in a faint black vanishing smudge, leaving the clear pure flame to dance alone.

N'mumba was appalled. The woman M'bu had cried the Prince's death, and now he knew the fabled tree had died as well. With a cry of dismay he rushed into her hut and saw her body on the ground. The Syrian stood over her, a knife red in his hand. Before anyone could seize him, others of M'bu's former slaves came to join him from the crowd, to hold off N'mumba and the tribe from vengeance. There were few of them, and they would have failed, if N'mumba hadn't been so torn and shaken by disaster that he could neither collect himself, nor give clear orders to anyone else.

He turned aside, ignoring the triumphant Syrian, and hurried to look for Meri-Mekhmet. He found her still quivering with terror on the pile of skins. With one glance he saw the guardian snake was dead. Something desperate had happened. All the magic of the tribe had perished together, blown away by a terrible wind from somewhere, as the smoke had been blown away by a terrible wind from somewhere, as the smoke had been blown from the fiery pillar into the enormous sky.

He flung himself on his face at Meri-Mekhmet's feet, crying: 'The gods of Kemi are stronger than the power of M'bu!'

Deep in the jungle Reuben's elephant raised his

trunk, and trumpeted a triumphant approach. All the way to the stockade, at intervals, he made this sound of glory.

Awaiting them at the entrance they found the whole tribe assembled, with N'mumba at its head; and as they came through the opening the frightened people fell flat upon the ground, leaving only the Syrian merchant, with the other former slaves, upright.

'Well,' said Cefalu, proudly erect on M'tuska's head, and curling his tail around his front paws, 'it has happened again, which is most gratifying. Do you remember, Master, how the High Priest of Sekhmet and all his friends fell on their faces before me in the desert, fearing I was sent by their goddess? However,' he added generously, 'it may be that some of this is due to you.'

'Cefalu,' responded Reuben sternly, as the elephant halted, 'it is due to neither of us, but to the great God of my fathers.' And Cefalu's ears and tail drooped with unaccustomed shame.

Now N'mumba rose to his feet and came forward, looking as though a hippopotamus had crushed him a second time. He recognized Reuben at once, and said gutturally but without expression, 'King of Kemi is revenged. My Prince is dead. Wise woman M'bu, with all magic of our tribe, is dead. Her tree is dead. So King of Kemi ruler here.'

'Where is the Princess Meri-Mekhmet?' demanded Reuben, almost afraid to ask.

Meri-Mekhmet had heard M'tuska's trumpeting as

192

he approached, but she had not known the sound, to her it was just one more thing to fear. The sudden silence when he entered the stockade had been terrifying. Then – was she hearing things, still enchanted? – she heard Reuben's voice. She listened while N'mumba spoke, and next time Reuben's words rang clear.

She gave a great cry of joy: 'Reuben! Oh Reuben – I am here!' Tears of thankfulness streamed down her face, and she ran from the hut towards him, her happiness as gay as the dancing flames that had eaten up the tree.

That night the tribe feasted Reuben as though he were their new ruler himself. Meri-Mekhmet, wearing a brilliant crown of jungle flowers, sat at his right hand, hardly able to believe he was there. A fire burnt in the centre of the stockade, and each time its flames died a little, and her tears could fall unnoticed, she wept from relief, careful nobody should see her. She was proud, as Tahlevi had once said.

After the feast there was dancing, with clapping of hands and rhythmic stamping of feet; and then the warriors danced alone, shaking their spears towards the ground, and crying 'Hieu- hieu!' as the long line swayed and curved in a fashion that reminded Reuben forcefully of a snake.

Later, when gourds of palm wine were being handed round for the fifth or sixth time, a solitary figure walked in and pushed its way to Reuben's side.

'So,' said Kenamut, with a slight snicker of complacency, 'We really managed well. Very creditable, my dear young friend. I hear – for these things get around, in the jungle – that you had the good fortune to kill some sort of snake, and the woman M'bu is dead, and the Prince unlikely to return. No doubt my King will properly show his gratitude! Ah, dear child,' he added, taking Meri-Mekhmet by the hand, and reminding her rather unfortunately, by the way he looked at her, of the Prince of Punt, 'my friend Reuben will have told you all we went through on your account! Action belonged to Reuben, but the worse, lonely danger of waiting in the jungle to keep rearward watch, belonged to me. Not that I claim credit, since this sort of cold courage is a natural gift. I see the place of honour is already occupied, so I shall arrange myself on your other side.'

He did so, carefully avoiding Cefalu, whose claws looked somewhat loosely sheathed.

'It may be her other side,' said Reuben drily, 'but at least you know now which one you're on.'

Throughout the evening N'mumba had stood apart, watching impassively his fellows feast this man who, by his great warm magic, had killed their Prince and their wise woman, reduced their strength, and humbled their pride. The jungle code held no place for sentiment. Win or lose, kill or be killed, do homage to the victor, despise the vanquished. All this he knew and accepted, but he had brought up the Prince as his own son since the former Prince had died, and the knife that pierced the woman

M'bu's heart might have pierced his also, so strong and terrible was his grief.

Much later, while the dancing continued, he moved to Reuben's elbow. 'Here dead Prince's nephew,' he said, thrusting a young boy forward. 'If King will, he make good Prince. And tell King, tribe he already punished, no need punish more.' Then N'mumba turned and walked from the stockade back along the half-hidden path to the creek, where he untied a small canoe and pushed out on to the stream in the direction of the wide lake where his Prince had died. He looked round him once at the land he had returned to joyously, and paddled away, and was never seen again.

No one was ever more delighted to leave prison than Meri-Mekhmet to leave that horrible stockade next day. She had slept in the main hut, tucked up with Cefalu on the pile of skins from which the dead snake had been removed. Reuben lay outside with M'tuska hobbled beside him, and all four were guarded by the released slaves whose spears – just in case – were well tipped with the same potent drug that had killed the great snake of the dreadful tree. No one knows what happened to the woman M'bu's body. That remains a tribal secret. Some say she was burnt, others that she was eaten, but whatever happened it's certain not much pleasure was gained from it.

Meri-Mekhmet had begged to leave for Kemi immediately. She hated to spend more time in that evil spot, but Reuben, although wrung by her distress, refused. They were all too tired, he said. Next day food would be provided by the tribe, and with the freed Syrian merchant they could start for home. Cefalu spoke kindly but firmly to her, as he would have done to Meluseth. Since owning Ptahsuti she understood cat language as well as Thamar did.

'It is all female whims and fancies,' he said, settling himself on her chest and tucking his paws in under him, 'for one grass hut is exactly like another, and the evil of this place is dead. You cannot deceive a cat. There's nothing here any more that could alarm a single mouse,' and he pumped his paws up and down to show her she could count on him, and also that she was not to move too much or he would be dislodged. So they slept, one comfortable and the other comforted.

The journey home was mostly uninteresting, which in real life is something to be thankful for. However, there was one incident which must be told. Kenamut had brooded enviously on what he thought of as Reuben's undeservedly easy success. The farther they got from the stockade, the more he regretted not taking a very active part, and the more he coveted all the King's gratitude for himself. They had stopped for a brief rest beside the last muddy creek before the jungle would be left behind. Logs floated on it, and the shores were strewn with boulders. While the Syrian snoozed and Meri-Mekhmet amused herself by plucking scarlet blossoms from a tree, Kenamut picked up one of Reuben's spears, and slyly approached as his back was turned and he was trying the creek water to see if it was drinkable. Luckily, he had just decided it was not, and swivelled round unexpectedly, to find the spear aimed at his heart. He cried out, attracting Meri-Mekhmet's attention, and at the same time leapt sideways with desert agility.

The very thrust Kenamut had given the weapon as it left his hand unbalanced him, and carried him a short way after it. While it fell harmlessly in the creek, Kenamut fell there to his hurt. He lay sprawled across a floating log. It moved. He struggled to rise, but the log was now swimming under him, and he could not regain his feet. He screamed for help, but none could come in time. The appalled watchers on the bank saw the crocodile bear him into midstream, and sink beneath him. There was a swirl of muddy water, a congregating of other logs, a flicker of brown waving arms, and a choked, water-swallowing cry. Kenamut had gone.

'*Oh* . . .' Meri-Mekhmet, pale as sand, clutched at Reuben's arm. 'Poor man . . . Poor horrible man. He was trying to kill you, and – ' She hid her face against Reuben's shoulder.

'The crocodiles might well have killed me.' Reuben spoke grimly, staring at the place where Kenamut had disappeared, now marked only by a brownish stain. 'What a fool I was – to trust this jungle, or Kenamut! I may have been too tired to know what I was doing, but that's no excuse a man should make for himself. The God of my fathers has saved me once again.' He put his arm around Meri-Mekhmet, and guided her gently back towards the elephant.

And after that they continued their journey, and no more evil happened to them on the way.

Homecoming and
Homegoing

'When will they come?' asked Meluseth fretfully, for
the hundredth time. She had given birth to one snow
white kitten, and her hold on life was frail. The kitten
had been born with good auguries, and was bound
to be exceptional. Its coat was short, sleek and daz-
zling, and unlike most kittens, who are born with
blue eyes, it had right from the start one green eye
and one blue. It was female, and was named Nutka.

'We don't know they will – ever again,' sighed
Thamar. She looked grave while she tried to feed
Meluseth with a little milk. She divided her time
between cat and King, coaxing both to eat, and doing
her best not to imagine dreadful things which could
have happened to Reuben. In public she kept a brave
face, but privately she despaired. It was so long since
the ship's Captain brought back news that Reuben
had met a stranger who could guide him to the
Prince's land. Long, since the Prince disappeared too
early. She was helped only by the King's comforting
words, which they both wanted so much to believe.

'You know how resourceful your husband is – how
can you doubt his return?' Merenkere asked with

mock severity; and she would retort: '*You* know how devoted to your Majesty Meri-Mekhmet is, and what a will she has. O Sovereign, my lord, how can you doubt she'll use it to escape?' Both pretended each had fooled the other.

'Besides, I think your husband is specially protected,' said Merenkere one morning, as he sat down suddenly on a chair. His legs gave frequently under him, although he now insisted on getting up a little every day, his bouts of fever notwithstanding.

Thamar silently nodded her head.

'How is Meluseth?'

'Weaker, your Majesty. She will not eat.'

The King looked grave. 'She pines for Cefalu. We should not have let him go.'

'We couldn't have stopped him, O Sovereign, my lord. He is an obstinate cat. Besides, he's very clever, and of use to Reuben. I do not think Meluseth pines – she has just lost interest in living. She feels her time is come. Animals are like that, I've seen it before. Her only pleasure is thinking of how much fuss may be made about embalming her. She would hate Cefalu to be absent, instead of following the procession to her tomb. It would not look well.'

'Even Benoni is depressed.' The King laid his hand on the herd dog's ruff. Benoni looked back out of anxious eyes. He was troubled by Reuben's absence – hurt, too, that only Cefalu had gone; and had almost decided to attach himself permanently to Merenkere. Anak was bitterness itself against elephants who oozed their way in when no one was looking.

In fact none of them were very happy; except down on the waterfront, where Khnum-Put smiled in his whiskers at the good turn he had done the strong and brilliant Prince of Punt.

That day there was a small stir in the streets. Hope was raised in everybody's heart. A heavily veiled woman was escorted into the city centre by a caravan from across the Nile, and was brought to the Palace where she demanded Thamar. But it proved not to be Meri-Mekhmet, only Noah's wife, who had always wanted to know what the women wore in that terrible idolatrous land of Kemi, and had slipped out one day when Noah was having a small celebration, and come to see. Her presence at least created a diversion. She was given audience of the King, prostrated herself with some difficulty and flutterings of the heart, rejoiced to see Thamar who was equally delighted to see her, condoled in the most comforting way over Reuben's perils, expressed herself shocked at everything she saw, and quickly acquired an almost transparent linen dress that would have made Noah thunder in his best prophetic vein. Then she was taken away and lodged with the priestess Tut, who could make nothing of her at all, and was indignant when her uninvited guest asked to spend all day seething herbs and lamb together in the kitchen. 'The idea!' said Tut. 'Everyone will leave.' And she tried to make Noah's wife shake a sistrum in the Temple, without success.

'Idolatry,' said Noah's wife, 'is what Noah would not have.' And she sat sulking in her linen dress,

and refusing to go home till Reuben and Meri-Mekhmet had returned.

So they were all getting very tired of waiting for the
wanderers, and waiting and waiting . . .

And Meluseth was tired of waiting too, and one
night died. The moon had risen. Meluseth dragged
herself to her feet, and tottered to the middle of the
floor.

'There is my old friend,' she told the anxious
Thamar, 'who used to visit me in my own Temple,
one queen calling upon another. How beautiful it is
to renew such bonds! I do not think Cefalu ever
understood the pearl he had acquired. It is the one
sorrow of my life, but we cannot all be nobly born,
and he tried hard. Remember me to him, and do not
let him bring the children up too coarsely.'

She shut her eyes in a great yawn – Thamar noticed
how small and triangular her face had grown – and
lay to sleep in a moony path of light. In the morning
she was cold. A cat of stone, in a coat of downy fur.
Thamar was very much upset. All the tears she had
kept back for Reuben came welling up ridiculously
for poor Meluseth. The King sent for Tahlevi, whose
robust common sense and perfect taste for the placing of jewels on the departed he hoped would comfort her.

They were all fussing over Meluseth, trying to
decide whether ropes of carnelian or turquoise bracelets looked best against her fur, and the kitten was
sitting on Noah's wife's knee for comfort, and the

Vizier Senusmet was looking at Noah's wife with some surprise – in fact, they were so absorbed that they failed to hear a commotion outside in the corridor. Suddenly, there was Reuben standing in the doorway, leading Meri-Mekhmet by the hand.

There was more commotion. Thamar flung herself into Reuben's arms, and the King seized Meri-Mekhmet in his.

'Oh, Merenkere!' said Meri-Mekhmet joyfully at last, when she could speak again, 'the Prince of Punt is dead, and the woman M'bu as well, and you are ruler of the whole tribe unless you let the Prince's nephew rule, of course, and I was bewitched but Reuben killed the snake with human eyes – '

'It all sounds confusing and quite horrible,' said the King, embracing her again, and leading her to a chair.

'Oh, horrible it was! You know, all the time I was so sorry that I ever went into the garden when you told me not to – '

'Which seems to me the most inadequate remark I ever heard!' Merenkere began to laugh. 'What a lot of trouble your disappearance has caused us all, my first sister – You owe – we all owe – an enormous debt to Reuben.'

'I know it.' Meri-Mekhmet held out a hand to Thamar. 'That you all suffered so much because of me makes me feel terrible.'

'Never mind, Princess.' Thamar emerged from Reuben's arms like someone coming out beneath a wave. 'Everything is perfect now.'

'Perfect!' Cefalu stood quivering at their feet, peering sadly across the room at the draped couch where Meluseth lay extended amongst turquoises and carnelian.

'Oh, Cefalu – '

'Poor Cefalu – '

'Everything we could do, was done – '

They were all ashamed of themselves.

'Leave me with her.' Cefalu pointedly ignored even the Sovereign.

That night he held a wake upon the Palace roof, where everyone who wished to come was invited. Ptahsuti was second mourner, but the new white kitten was deemed too young. There was such a wailing and a throbbing as had never before been heard in the city of Men-nofer, not even on the waterfront. It almost extinguished the stars. Everyone knew something terrible had happened, and many stayed indoors or sent offerings to the temples. From this catharsis Cefalu emerged with the controlled grief of the born bachelor.

The High Priest of Ptah wished to conduct the rite of opening the mouth and ears of the dead, when the time came. She would then hear and speak, he said, in the hereafter. But Cefalu put down his paw. 'It is not only against true religion,' he argued, 'but common sense. It is stupid to open the female mouth, quite unnecessary too.' However, he allowed a charm against serpents to be placed in the tomb, as a concession to Meluseth's upbringing in Kemi, together with a sistrum presented by the priestess

Tut, carved with the likenesses of Ptahsuti and Nutka. Meri-Mekhmet and the King gave a small gold couch.

It has been said a happy woman has no history: yet Meri-Mekhmet was only embarking on hers, as wife of the greatest monarch of that time. Those incidents which had made her life so frightening were over, and Merenkere was well again, now she had returned. No longer was there danger from Kemi's Vizier, for Senusmet was tamed. No one had quite known what to do with Noah's wife, who kept putting off her journey home in order to buy dresses, and collect rich green and blue glazed pottery, and wine cups for Noah of deep blue shaped like the calyx of the lotus flower. At last they lodged her with the Vizier, as official guest, where they hoped the strain would make her leave. But Noah's wife found her way to his kitchens, and discovered the art and joy of seething waterfowl in herbs. All day long she cooked up such delicious food that his table became famous, and he himself seldom left his house in case he missed something.

Noah's wife was not in the least scared of his tantrums. She had had all that with Ham. She would just cluck her tongue, and say: 'Fancy, now – ' or 'So sharp, you'll cut yourself – ' or 'You men will always use your brains,' in such a disparaging way that soon he was unable to, and merely sat about the house waiting to be fed, so that the King very nicely and quietly suggested he might now retire.

'You must be my Vizier instead,' he told Reuben.

'O Sovereign, my lord!' Reuben was aghast, 'I know nothing of government.'

'That might well be good, seeing what happens when people govern who do know.' The King laughed. 'But I see your point. You have accomplished miracles, and it is unfair to expect them all the time.' So he appointed a young man called Hekh, handsome, brilliant, full of integrity, and so in love with Meri-Mekhmet he was no trouble to anyone at all. In fact, the only outstanding problem they had left was cleaning up the waterfront under Khnum-Put's rule.

This, Cefalu made his business, once he emerged from mourning. He had just paid Meluseth's tomb an official visit, to see how the wall paintings were getting on, and to approve the inscription on the south wall of the inner chamber which would contain her bronze coffin when her embalming was complete. She had dictated the words to Thamar some time before she died.

'The Eternal House of Meluseth, She Who Loves the Moon. I was the honour of my sister Sekhmet, a fragrant guardian of the Two Lands. In the Temple I failed not in my duties, the Sovereign rejoiced to see my power and nimbleness in his service. Greatness did not spoil my humility, nor the blinding radiance of my Self lead to pride and vainglory. In the Ark I was an example to all, exerting myself constantly for the common good. A fine mouser, noble mother, and tireless mate, I present myself modestly to the judgement of Re.'

Cefalu wiped his eyes with a paw after Reuben read him this, and was silent for some time, and then said he felt like a good fight. He took a guard of faithful Palace cats and, from the double wall, issued a challenge demanding Khnum-Put should come and fight it out.

'A traitor shall not rule in Men-nofer,' spat Cefalu.

There was a pause, while this insulting message was carried to the waterfront.

Back came the answer. Khnum-Put would fight if Cefalu would do battle with only three legs.

'One back leg is already bandaged to my body,' replied Cefalu.

There was a second pause. Then, out of the dark, came Khnum-Put. His good eye pierced the gloom with a glow of fire.

'I will close one eye,' called Cefalu provocatively. 'Come up here, O Khnum-Put, and leave your guard behind. Mine is below me in the garden.'

What a battle that was! It is recorded in many wall-paintings, and was even enamelled on Meluseth's coffin. Bits of the double wall were scarred and disfigured; here and there bricks were torn out bodily, and were left missing to mark the famous battle. A branch of the tamarisk was scored from end to end, while both cats lost so much fur that parts of them were almost bald.

Suddenly the two prancing, yowling shadows locked in combat fell apart. One of them tottered slightly. A ball of bleeding fur tumbled with a terrible thud from the outer wall, and lay silent for a moment.

The other shadow peered unbelievingly down. Would the combat be renewed . . . ? No: to a hissing and groaning from his followers Khnum-Put rose dizzily on to three paws, and limped very slowly and beatenly away.

'Tribute tomorrow to the Palace,' called Cefalu, and, amid rejoicing, dragged his punished body back to Reuben's and Thamar's quarters, and their bed.

Next day a large mouse signed with Khnum-Put's abdication was received in the Palace of White Walls. He was never seen again on the waterfront. It is rumoured he retired into a temple, and spent his last years meditating.

News of this abdication was brought to the King and Meri-Mekhmet while they were still receiving tribute prior to their marriage, which couldn't take place till the Great Royal Wife had been buried with due ceremony in her tomb. Many beautiful objects had arrived from the new young Prince of Punt, collected from his whole kingdom, not just its steamy heart of rulership. There were fans of ostrich feather; carved ivory, gold inlaid; panther skins; and great caskets of sandalwood containing precious myrrh and incense. Meri-Mekhmet could not look at them without a shudder.

'Will not Thamar accept some of this?' the King asked Reuben. 'Meri-Mekhmet is upset by it.'

'O my lord the King, I will ask her, just to please you. But your Majesty knows we have not wanted a reward.'

'Yes, I know.' Merenkere looked his exasperation.

'My friend, why can you not be like other men? You make me quite uncomfortable. No high office – no jewels, lands, rings of gold. Surely a little sandalwood – '

'A little!'

Reuben went away to ask Thamar's opinion. He returned with a message. 'O Sovereign, my lord, my wife thanks the King for his great goodness, but – '

'Refuses? What a pair. I will put you both in prison.'

Reuben grinned. 'Spare us, O my Sovereign, I beg of you. Thamar hesitantly asked if you would kindly make a present of it to Tahlevi. He could keep whatever was of use to him and barter the rest for jewels. It would greatly please us both.'

'If this is the only way I may reward you obstinate people, I will do so. But it annoys me, and makes me want to wring your necks.'

Reuben laughed aloud. 'O Sovereign, my lord, all we need is your and Princess Meri-Mekhmet's friendship. After all, I have my lands in Canaan.'

The King looked at him, and groaned. 'This means you want to go there.'

'Not want, my lord the King. It's my duty to go there, and restore them to what they were before the Flood. Through Noah my God has given them to me, and so I must see they flourish. Then – if your Majesty allows it – we shall return.'

'Go,' said the King in extreme exasperation, but shaking Reuben in a friendly manner by the shoulder, 'I never thought to like best in my Kingdom the one man in it whom I could not rule! Yet whether you like it or not, I shall give you and Thamar everything you need to start your life in Canaan, and a great feast besides, before you go. And, since my new Vizier's settled in his office, and my remarkable Senusmet's teeth are drawn, it is time you took Mother Noah with you, for she shows a marked reluctance to leave, and her poor old husband must be lost without her.'

So it was settled, and there was a great feast before they left. Everyone was there, which means everyone who counted in the Two Lands, and some who didn't. Aunt Tut was there, in her state of constant ecstasy since it was sure Meri-Mekhmet would marry with the King, and irritating her brother the Court Chamberlain Ay by saying she had always said so, which was untrue. Tahlevi was there, since the ex-Vizier Senusmet was confined to bed with a stomach upset; and Cefalu and Benoni (who was delighted to be with Reuben again, and had forgotten his jealousy) represented the animals. Anak and M'tuska took umbrage, in spite of a splendid entertainment for larger beasts in the Palace outbuildings, and being fully aware there was no room for them inside.

'When they want us to carry something, you will see how popular we shall become,' said Anak sourly.

They soon were wanted to carry something. It was a tremendous procession which started out for Canaan. King Merenkere had fulfilled his threat (or promise), and more and more donkeys were gradually added to those carrying what he had already given Reuben and Thamar. They were overwhelmed, and gave up protesting. They simply accepted everything, their eyes large with astonishment. Urns of alabaster, stools of gold, mountains of foodstuffs, rugs and linen; and wine from the King's vineyards, and tame birds for breeding, and every form of plant and seed that could start a new land growing. And the King gave Reuben servants, and Thamar maid-servants, and cattle and sheep and goats. And a scribe who could write to tell him all they were doing, and when they were coming back.

'Goodbye!' cried Meri-Mekhmet, waving from the Palace outer court, with Ptahsuti in her arms.

'Goodbye, O Sovereign, goodbye, Princess Meri-Mekhmet!' called Reuben and Thamar, waving from Anak and M'tuska.

Benoni wagged his tail while trotting in the dust, but Cefalu, riding on M'tuska's head in all the splendour of his bandages, merely moved a languid paw in farewell.

King Merenkere raised the kitten with different-coloured eyes so that she could see her father go. He had asked to keep her as a companion for Ptahsuti. But the kitten was not at all interested in her father, who had been away when she was born. She was staring up into the brilliant, dazzlingly fresh sky, where a hawk hovered above the departing guests. She would have liked to put out a paw and catch it.

Reuben saw it too, and raised his hand, and pointed, and looked back at Merenkere with a smile. For a moment, as Anak ambled clumsily along, the shadow of wings came between him and the sun; but this time, when Reuben saw it as he had seen it on his first journey as a prisoner to Kemi, he knew it for a shadow of benevolence, a blessing; a sign of the true bond that existed between himself and Thamar and the King – the Horus of Gold.

'I cannot bear to see them go,' sighed Meri-Mekh-met, almost in tears.

'Come back into the Palace, my first sister,' said the King.